Wolftalker

Book Three
of
The Naming of Brook Storyteller

by
Ghillian Potts

ARACHNE PRESS

First published in UK 2018 by Arachne Press Limited
100 Grierson Road, London SE23 1NX
www.arachnepress.com
© Ghillian Potts 2018
ISBNs
Print, 978-1-909208-49-0
Mobi/Kindle 978-1-909208-51-3
ePub 978-1-909208-50-6

Printed on wood-free paper in the UK by TJ International, Padstow.

WOLFTALKER

Also by Ghillian Potts
The Old Woman from Friuli

The Naming of Brook Storyteller
Book One: *Brat*
Book Two: *Spellbinder*

CHAPTER ONE

Storyteller Wolftalker Dragonfriend had found it difficult to persuade her friend to wait for her outside the village of Edgescarp. 'I'm sorry,' she told him, 'but they'll be scared of you, too scared to listen to me. I'll be perfectly safe here, you know. It's only a small place. Just wait till I call you.'

The huge wolf grumbled low in his throat and reluctantly sat down to wait.

Wolftalker clucked to her pony and rode slowly into the village. She must get this story right. At least one youngster's happiness – possibly his life – depended on it. And she had to tell the village why it had been left so long untold.

She knew she looked too young to be telling the villagers anything important. So she rode casually into the village square that evening, looking confident and calm. She was obviously a storyteller. Her hair was a little short for one of their women but her clothes – ankle boots and riding breeches under a long tunic – were well fitting and of good cloth and she wore a scarf of storyteller-blue around her neck.

Everyone began to gather round, wondering who she was and whether she was really alone and all the other things villagers always want to know about a stranger.

The storyteller sat there on her small rough pony, smiling a little, saying nothing until all the talk died down.

Then, 'Elders of Edgescarp, may I speak to all the folk?'

There was an odd silence. This was something unusual and small places like Edgescarp don't like strangeness. Then old One-eye, holder of the best fields around, stepped forward.

'You have a message, Storyteller...?'

She ignored the little pause left for her name.

The crowd thickened and pressed closer. Storytellers set great store by their names. Here was something else out of place.

The storyteller looked all round her, then began to speak into their waiting silence.

'For now my name does not matter. I am the Voice of Storyteller Silkentongue, the Storyteller of the Joined Lands,' she said.

There was a gasp. Everyone knew the name of the finest and most important storyteller in the land, Court Storyteller to the Overlord himself. How had he ever heard of one small, unimportant village?

'Storyteller Silkentongue wishes to apologise on behalf of all storytellers to the village of Edgescarp and particularly to one family in this village and to one member of that family.'

She paused again, waited for the hissing whispers to die out and went on: 'To the boy Cricket, to his father and mother and all their family, to all their friends and neighbours in this village, Storyteller Silkentongue and the Guild of Storytellers of the Joined Lands offer this apology for the wrongsaying of Gaingold Storyteller.' She swallowed, looking around to catch all eyes. 'We are deeply ashamed that one of our guild should unjustly have scorned and humiliated you and yours and we beg you to pardon us. What amends may be made, I, as the Voice of Silkentongue, am here to attempt, by your leaves.' She paused, looking from one to another. 'May I speak first to Cricket?'

Cricket had tried to hang back. He wanted to hate all storytellers but the pull of the storytelling was as strong as ever and he could not walk away. Indeed, his parents pushed him forward through the crowd as soon as the storyteller pronounced his name and by the time she had finished, he was standing at the pony's side. Wolftalker looked down at him and smiled.

'You are Cricket, of course. Will you accept our apology?'

He couldn't speak. He nodded, his teeth in his lip.

6

Then everyone was cheering and patting the boy on the back, and Wolftalker leaned down to him from the pony's back.

'Cry if you need to,' she said into his ear. 'I'll distract them,' and before he could begin to feel indignant, she had slid from the pony's back and was asking if she might call her escort.

'I knew they'd never let a child like that come by herself!' said somebody.

'Please, everyone,' said the storyteller, 'don't be scared. I promise there is no danger,' and she gave a long high call, almost like a hawk's scream.

Into the square trotted the huge grey wolf.

There was a mass movement away. Someone began to mutter about spears, a girl screamed and a small boy started to cry. Then Wolftalker called to the wolf in Elder tongue and he sat down, looking about alertly and lolling out his tongue. All the dogs of the village were barking hysterically but the wolf paid no attention.

Cricket gave his eyes a quick scrub while everyone was, as the storyteller had promised, distracted and wondered if she had not overdone it.

She strolled over to the wolf and sat down beside him in the roadway, an arm about his neck. The dogs fell gradually silent.

'This is my friend Drinks-the-Wind,' she told them. 'He is a Wildron wolf from Gilden Forest and he travels with me when he feels like it. He will not harm you or your beasts, I promise.'

'Does he do tricks?' asked one of the bolder boys.

'Stars, no! He is his own wolf, not mine. I would never ask him to lower himself. No, I am the one who does tricks,' and Wolftalker laughed so infectiously that they all found themselves laughing too.

'I have discharged one half of my obligation,' she said when they were quiet again. 'The other half depends upon Cricket.'

She turned to the boy and spoke very soberly. 'Cricket? You have forgiven us: and we are deeply indebted to you. I must ask you now. Do you still wish to become a Storyteller?'

CHAPTER TWO

Everyone fell silent.

Cricket longed to yell at them, 'Haven't you anything better to do than stare at me?'

The storyteller was watching him, too.

It was no use trying to pretend. He felt a huge grin stretching his mouth and suddenly he shouted 'Yes! Oh yes!' and found himself being hugged by all his relations, some of whom had barely spoken to him for a year.

When Cricket fell out of the whirlpool of congratulations, he found the storyteller beside him, smiling.

'I still have to test you, Cricket,' she warned him, 'but if Storyteller Spring Rain felt confident enough to promise to sponsor you, I don't think you need worry.'

Rain! He had not forgotten her, although in his bitterness he had tried to, telling himself that she had only amused herself and was probably glad not to have to bother with him.

Now he grabbed the storyteller's arm eagerly. Then let go in a hurry as the wolf's low growl warned him off.

'Have you seen her? How is she? Gaingold Storyteller said she was senile and would die soon – tell me, please!' he begged.

'Gaingold.' Her mouth twisted as if she had tasted acid. 'Spring Rain is well and has gone to live in a village called Brownhill. I'll take you there as soon as I can manage it. She has a tiny house and is as happy as she can be without her husband. Speakwell's death was hard for her. Her sister's youngest grandson and his wife live next door and all their children are in and out all day. I went to see her on my way here, so my news is fresh. How do you think we knew where to find you?'

She smiled back at his grin of relief then pulled her face straight. 'Come, Cricket,' she said sternly, 'let us find a quiet corner for your testing.'

Cricket was exhausted by the time she had done with him. He had to tell her tales and stories, in exactly the words of Spring Rain or Speakwell; he had to tell her one of his own tales – he asked her how she knew he had any of his own and her mouth curled into a smile – and finally, he had to tell, to the whole village, a story which she had only just told him. She instructed him to alter the tone of the story without changing any facts at all and without making it in any way untrue.

How Cricket sweated. It was dark when he finished and the bonfire his parents had provided in the square was burning low. The whole village was there to hear him and he peered anxiously from face to face in the flickering red light when he had reached the end, wondering what they thought of him. He did not dare to wonder what *she* thought.

'Have you any ale to toast our newest apprentice storyteller?' she said, laughing. And the congratulations began all over again.

Cricket's father was a sober man who liked to get every fact straight in his mind. He came across to them and stood staring at the storyteller.

'Storyteller, I am proud that my son should have been accepted by you but, your pardon, you are a young lass and –' he hesitated, trying so hard to be tactful that he was dumbstruck.

She looked up at him and said at once, 'You feel that I may be exceeding my authority, Farmer Broadleaf?' Her voice was so clear and carrying that everyone listened to her, whatever she said.

So all the village heard her say, 'I have not yet told you my name. I am Storyteller Wolftalker Dragonfriend.'

Cricket had never before heard a silence like that for any naming.

He knew that everyone here was remembering the story that Gaingold had told them of how Storyteller Spellbinder lost her

Name and was given two new ones: 'Wolftalker' by the Wilders, and, by the Young Overlord, 'Dragonfriend'. Gaingold had made a mock of her. He had made them believe she was a shame to all storytellers. And now here she was.

This was the storyteller who had lost her Name.

Much as Cricket had hated Gaingold and knew him for an envious and spiteful creature, he was so used to believing that storytellers always told the truth, that he had never thought to doubt this version of the story.

And indeed, Gaingold had not told them one word of a lie... But there are ways of telling the truth that are as near to a lie as you would wish to come. He had done his best to poison the story for them and for no reason but his own jealous spite.

Wolftalker looked round at them and said quietly, 'I see that an unfriend has been telling you my Story. May I tell it to you again?'

Cricket was later to hear this Story told many times but never so calmly and so straightforwardly as Wolftalker told it now. She made no attempt to win their pity for the girl child she had been when Arrow, Overlord of Westfold, threatened, not her life, but the lives of little children, storyteller children, unless she did his bidding. She made nothing of the desperate resolve of that child, to die beneath the Dragons' claws sooner than betray her own people.

'But when it came to the point,' she said quietly, 'and I was face to face with the Dragons, I could not do it. I chose to command them instead. And yet, had I only known it, I was perfectly safe. I would not have died, for the Dragons do not kill. But also, I could not have kept my word to Arrow. The Dragons would never have attacked the Joined Lands. I lost my Name for nothing, for a stupid misunderstanding.

'Make no mistake, I broke my vow to Arrow and he kept his to me. He freed the storytellers and their children and let them go unharmed, as he had promised. I did break my word. And so I lost the Name that I had pledged.'

Cricket could not hear the smallest tremble in her tone but he couldn't believe that the most light-hearted among the villagers did not feel the agony of her loss. To lose your name, even one given casually by friends, is bad enough: men had killed themselves for it, but to lose the Name given you by the Storyteller himself, the Name you gained when you were made a Master in your guild, that was to be flayed alive and every day have salt rubbed into the raw flesh.

Cricket hated Gaingold all over again. This time it was for Wolftalker, not himself. How could Gaingold add to her pain by his malice? He found he was clenching his fists as if to smash them into that venomous mouth.

'But, Storyteller, did the Dragons not attack Arrow's army and save the Joined Lands? How could they do it if they never kill?' protested Cricket's grandfather.

Wolftalker smiled at him. 'Why, since the soldiers believed that the Dragons would tear them to pieces, they ran in terror as soon as the Air Dragon flew at them. He had no need to touch them. They destroyed themselves.'

'Serve them right,' shouted someone from the crowd and everyone joined in, cheering Dragonfriend and the Dragons. She shook her head sadly, then she set herself to smile and be gracious until, all the food eaten and all the ale drunk, everyone went happily to bed.

Next morning, clutching a hastily assembled bundle of clothes and riding behind Wolftalker on her pony, Cricket set out to become a storyteller.

CHAPTER THREE

Cricket felt such a mixture of excitement at leaving, misery at parting from his family and nervousness of the strangeness he was going to, that for a good while he was silent.

They jolted along at a brisk trot, the wolf ranging now ahead, now beside them, then dropping back as if to check for followers. Wolftalker Dragonfriend was as quiet as the boy.

At last, she twisted around and asked, 'How are you doing, Cricket? You can't be very comfortable. Shall we walk for a bit?'

Cricket came back to himself with a start. She was quite right: he was very uncomfortable.

'I'm not used to riding,' he confessed. 'I never was on a pony before. We don't use them for riding.'

Wolftalker pulled up. 'I thought you'd like to make a grand exit,' she said, grinning at him over her shoulder, 'but now we're well away, we can take it in turn to ride. Hop down and try your legs. Here, give me the bundle. No need to carry it yourself. Marker won't even notice it.'

Cricket's legs felt weak and he had to hang on to the saddle for a moment but pushed away quickly, hoping she hadn't seen. Wolftalker Dragonfriend let the pony amble along slowly until he had limbered up, then they went on as fast as Cricket comfortably could.

'Where are we going?' he asked at last. He had no idea, apart from the generally south-westerly direction of this ridge road. He had never before been anywhere but to the market town, Underhill, lying almost due north of Edgescarp.

'In the end, to the City,' said Wolftalker. She chuckled at Cricket's gasp of awe. 'For now, we are on our way to Scarp-end, to buy you a pony. We should get there in a couple of days at this rate. Unfortunately, there's nowhere nearer. I could have brought another mount with me but you might have turned me down, mightn't you? And I did not want to appear too confident.'

'You mean you were worried I'd refuse?' He could not believe it. 'You? Afraid of us thinking...' Cricket trailed off, confused.

Wolftalker looked down at him, her face serious. 'Listen to me carefully, Cricket Storyteller,' she said. 'Gaingold Storyteller dishonoured all storytellers by his treatment of you. Had you refused our apology and decided not to accept our offer, how could we have made good our honour? Why do you think I was sent, not any other? I am the Young Overlord's Remembrancer and her Court Storyteller; my great uncle Silkentongue is the Storyteller; I have two Names, both of them honourable even if I did lose my first storyteller Name. I am needed in the City at this moment, yet this mission was so important to our guild that Storyteller Silkentongue insisted that I must come. He would have come himself but that he is ill.'

Cricket stood still in the road and stared at her. He looked around him as if the rock face on the right and the drop on his left, the trees and bushes, even the packed earth beneath his feet might have changed. But they were just the same. It was Cricket who had changed.

He said stupidly: 'I shan't be able to ride very fast, I don't suppose.'

'Huh?' Wolftalker shook her head bemusedly, then laughed. 'Because I said I am needed in the City? Don't fret yourself. There is not that much haste. You can be learning something of riding on the way to Scarp-end. Most of this road is too rough and steep for travelling at more than a walk anyway.'

On they went. After a little, Wolftalker gave Cricket a riding lesson, walking beside him, telling him how to hold the reins and, more importantly, his body. Marker plodded along and Cricket began to feel secure on his back, even swaggering a little inside.

He fell gradually into a daydream of riding home one day, not on a little rough pony but on a tall horse, which would gallop into the village street; the sort of horse on whose back one could outpace the wind or fight a dragon. He was wondering how it felt to confront a dragon as Dragonfriend had done and whether he would bear himself as well as she had, when she startled him out of it.

'Hey! Cricket! You can't daydream on horseback.'

She caught Marker's rein and Cricket realised that they were right on the edge of the road. The drop below was not all that great, but to Cricket at that moment it looked like a mile.

Wolftalker frowned at him, then, seeing his hands shaking, she said in a milder tone, 'Well, that's one mistake you'll not make again. I should have been more alert myself. Whatever were you thinking of?'

Cricket swallowed. 'I was thinking about – well, glory. And the Elder Dragons. Shall I ever see them, do you suppose?' he said in a rush, wondering if she minded talking about them.

'I shouldn't think so. They have gone back to sleep and no one would summon them save for a very great need,' said Wolftalker. 'It might happen, one day; but it is very unlikely.'

'Oh.' Cricket was not sure whether he was relieved or disappointed. 'Are they very terrifying?'

'Very. When I first saw one, I was so scared I wet my pants,' Wolftalker told him cheerfully.

Cricket gasped, choked and then snickered helplessly, all his heroic fantasies vanishing. And Wolftalker Dragonfriend, the Young Overlord's Court Storyteller, laughed with him.

Between Edgescarp and Scarp-end, Cricket asked hundreds of questions about the storytellers and storytelling; a question for every stone in their path all the length of that rocky mountain road, claimed Wolftalker. She was amazingly patient with him; and he asked even more questions.

He did not know it at the time, but she was teaching him all the things that young storytellers normally pick up from their kin and take for granted. If he had not asked, she would have told him all the same, he learned the faster for asking.

CHAPTER FOUR

They reached the town of Scarp-end in mid-afternoon of the second day, bought some supplies and a pony and its gear and went on.

Cricket had expected a halt in the town, perhaps for Wolftalker to tell some stories, but she barely paused long enough to bargain, paying more for the pony than Cricket was sure the dealer had dreamed of getting. They did not so much as eat their lastmeal at the inn, though Cricket, having never had a meal in a public eating house, was childishly disappointed and sulked silently as they set out again.

Wolftalker noticed the sulking but she paid no attention. Instead, for the first time she gave him a formal lesson.

'Now that we can converse instead of calling back and forth,' she said, reining Marker alongside Cricket's quiet pony, 'I can tell you the first Story that all apprentices are told. It is never told to any but Storytellers. Listen and remember, Storyteller to be, and in your turn you shall tell this story to your apprentice.'

And she told Cricket the Story of Nameless, the Master Storyteller once named Clevertongue, who was cast out by his guild and by his own mother for telling Stories which were not Stories but lies. He had been totally outcast, for, said Wolftalker, 'none of the folk, when they had heard the Story of Nameless, would speak one word to him or sell him food or give him shelter. With all his wealth about him, he died in a ditch, of hunger and cold and despair.

'As for his mother, who for shame had renounced even her Name, she wandered from one group of storytellers to another, always revered and honoured, speaking with them in the Elder tongue but never telling a story until at last she came to the Old Forest in the land of Captal. Here she stayed, living with the Wilders, who speak only the Elder tongue; and here she was given a Name again, for the Wilders, who call the wolves their cousins, Named her Wolftalker because she would sit in the forest and tell tales to the wolves.

'But no Storyteller since that time has ever been named Clevertongue,' finished Wolftalker.

'Is that why you...' Cricket began. And broke off, abashed.

'Yes, the Wilders gave me her name. One of them found me in the Gilden Forest telling this very Story to my friend Drinks-the-Wind.'

She nodded at the huge wolf who was ranging well ahead of them, since Cricket's pony objected strenuously to his presence.

'He'll have to get used to Drinks-the-Wind sooner or later,' she had remarked when they bought his mount, 'but we'll let them get acquainted gradually.'

So the wolf kept his distance, staying downwind as far as possible and the pony, a sturdy bay with a white star on his forehead, snorted less loudly and tossed his head less nervously each time Drinks-the-Wind came a little closer or the wind changed and brought him the wolf scent.

'You have two names,' Cricket said carefully. 'Should I use both, or do you prefer one?'

'In the City I am Dragonfriend, for that is the name The Young Overlord gave me; elsewhere, mostly I am Wolftalker, except amongst my closest friends, of course.' She grinned and would be drawn no further, and turning her attention to Cricket's pony announced that he should be Baylock, and when Cricket asked her why she smiled.

'It is the name by which I first knew Farwalker,' she told him.

'Lord Farwalker? The Archer?' Cricket was enthralled. 'Will he mind your calling a pony by his name?'

'No, of course not. Farwalker is not the sort to bother about an old use-name. I'm the only one who ever uses it nowadays, unless Gray still does. I don't know for sure because I have been in Gilden Forest with the Wilders since the Dragons went back to their slumber and I only returned to court a month ago; and then I was sent to find you almost at once.'

She looked suddenly sad. 'Farwalker was away visiting his landholding so I haven't seen him since the proclamation of the new Overlord of Westfold. Nearly a year, now.'

Cricket desperately wanted to know about the new Overlord of Westfold, about living with the Wilders and about Lord Farwalker's use-name and how Wolftalker had first met him; and who did she mean by 'Gray'? But he didn't dare ask.

'I'll tell you the story of my meeting with Gray and Baylock tonight when we've made camp,' she told him, as if she had read his mind. 'We'll have to stop soon. You can't make camp in the dark, but you can tell stories.'

CHAPTER FIVE

They were two weeks on the road altogether. In that time Wolftalker taught Cricket the Elder tongue. She forced him to learn very short tales and rhymes in that language. They were baby tales, simple, repetitive and easy to memorise, even before he understood them.

After the first week she refused to speak to him in the Common tongue at all, except to translate each tale once and once only.

By the time they reached the City, Cricket was dreaming in the Elder tongue and could carry on a simple conversation. He had also learned the Story of Nameless in that tongue. He discovered that in telling it to him in the Common tongue, Wolftalker had had to translate as she went.

'It is told only to storytellers, you see,' she explained, 'and so it is always told in our own language. The Wilders, as I told you, are the only other people who speak it all the time. Very few of them even now speak any of the Common tongues.'

'I didn't know there was more than one,' Cricket said, puzzled.

Wolftalker laughed. 'We of the Joined Lands claim that ours is the original one and all others are distorted versions of it. If so, some of them are very twisted indeed. The lands closest to us have more or less the same speech. You would have no difficulty in following what a Westfolderman said, for instance; but if you tried to talk to the people who live in the Desert Plains I doubt if you'd understand a word. They have so many different names for things that I can't believe their language ever came from ours at all.

'Still, words do change their meaning and even their sound over many years. Some of the Great Cycle Stories are very hard to understand. We Storytellers keep them unaltered for ourselves but we have to change some words so that folk nowadays know what they mean. It is a very solemn business, deciding to change even one word of the Great Cycle and there is always a long discussion between all the Master Storytellers and messages have to go to all the lands where they speak our version of the Common tongue and – oh, it is a great bore! I had to attend such a meeting just before I came to fetch you, Cricket. I promise you, if it had gone on much longer I'd have... well, I don't know what, but something unbecoming and violent. Don't ever tell anyone I said so, will you? It was a great honour.'

She pulled a wry face that made Cricket snort with laughter and promise never to let anyone know.

'But I should think they'd guess if you looked like that during the discussions,' he told her.

The City lay in the valley of the Great River. Above it the river divided, to join again below so that the City sat on an island. It was a tall island; the highest point, where the keep was, stood almost as high as the valley walls.

There was a story about the keep. It was intended to be taller than the valley's sides so that a lookout might be kept over the lands either side of the river; but the Overlord who ordered it built was a cruel man who was feared and hated by his people. They did not want to be overlooked. When the keep was nearly tall enough, therefore, the stone masons declared that the foundations were not deep enough to support the weight of another course. They refused to set one more stone upon another. The Overlord had their leader killed but still they refused. He tried to make others do the work but everyone believed, or else pretended to believe, the masons and at last he was obliged to roof his keep as it was. It still had an odd, unfinished look.

This was not something Cricket noticed that first time, of course. He just stood and stared down at the river, the bridges, great and small, crossing it, the wharves lining its banks and the City rising directly up behind them in tiers of houses.

'I first saw it from the other side where the river is wider but not so deep,' said Wolftalker. 'There are no wharves there but there are two fords and so, for safety, the City wall runs along the water's edge. It appears to grow out of the river. But I like this approach just as well.'

She held out her hands as if to cup the City lovingly between them. 'I don't regard it as my private property as I think my friend Strongtower does,' she added, grinning sideways at him, 'but I do like to come back to it. And Graycat is here. And perhaps Farwalker will be back by now.'

They were to enter the City by the northernmost bridge. This was the only one to lead directly into the City. It was very high, built out from a spur of rock in the valley wall. It arched over the valley, which was very narrow there, right over the river and the wharves, to an entrance gate about halfway up the island's side. The drop was enough to make Cricket dizzy.

All the bridges had a wooden drawbridge in the middle, a removable span which, on the lower bridges, was raised to allow ships to sail by. It could be taken away altogether in case of attack, although there had been no need to use this safeguard for many years. Even in the great invasion by the Westfoldermen, thirty years before, no enemy got near the City.

Drinks-the-Wind didn't like crossing the echoing wood of the drawbridge and hesitated, whining, at the edge. Wolftalker at once dismounted and went back to him. She knelt beside him and coaxed him gently, telling him that he had crossed it before and nothing had happened; but he still refused to move.

Suddenly she stood up and shouted to Cricket.

'Quickly! Get the ponies off! Everybody stand still!' She whirled on the people coming up behind them, holding out her arms to halt them. A cart was moving still and she yelled at the carter to stop. By this time Cricket was beside her, bewildered and beginning to think she had gone crazy. The carter, a lean, fierce woman, braked her huge cart and jumped down.

'Stark!' called Dragonfriend. 'Thank the Stars it's you! Don't let anyone on to the drawbridge. It's about to fall. I must stop the folk at the other end.'

Before the carter could reply, Dragonfriend turned and ran, fast and lightly across the very span she claimed would fall.

Drinks-the-Wind gave a great howl of distress and bounded after her. Cricket started to follow and Stark grabbed his shoulder. She held it so hard that he thought her fingers would meet through it.

'You heard what she said,' she told him. 'Stay.'

She might have been speaking to a dog. He stayed.

There was a splendidly dressed man on a big horse just about to move onto the drawbridge from the City end, with a group of men at arms behind him. Dragonfriend reached him as his horse balked, snorting and wild-eyed. The man, obviously thinking that she had alarmed his mount, shouted at her to get out of his way.

Dragonfriend stood still, right under the horse's nose. She had not yet stepped off the wooden span. By her side, Drinks-the-Wind whined anxiously.

'Lord, you must go back. The drawbridge is rotten. Your horse knows and is afraid.' Her voice was as clear and carrying as usual but Cricket could hear the waver in it. She was scared, too.

The lord peered at her. 'Moon and sun! It's Storyteller Dragonfriend! Rotten, you say? Can't see any signs of it, but if you say so,' he shrugged, waved back his men and started to back his horse off the wood.

As he did so, there was a groan from the timbers and someone yelled. Drinks-the-Wind sprang snarling against Dragonfriend, sending her staggering forward onto the safe stone portion of the bridge. Behind her, the drawbridge collapsed, crashing and thudding down to the river and the rocks below.

Cricket screamed. Drinks-the-Wind, off balance after

thrusting Dragonfriend to safety, was sliding backwards off the broken span. He scrabbled desperately but his hind legs were already hanging in space and he could get no purchase with his front claws.

Dragonfriend scrambled round on all fours and flung herself down beside him, reaching frantically for his ruff to try to lift him. It was hopeless, of course; she was nothing like strong enough. Cricket knew her well enough by now to be certain that she would fall with the wolf rather than let go.

'Help her!' he yelled at the top of his voice: 'Get ropes! Use your belts, reins, anything to lift the wolf!'

The lord dragged his horse's bridle over its head and his men began to unbuckle belts and empty their carrysacks in search of rope but they were all so slow!

Cricket whispered: 'Oh hurry, be quick, hurry up!' Afterwards, he found that he had dug his fingernails right through the skin of his palms.

Then a man in the Overlord's black and silver livery shot through the crowd and threw himself down beside Dragonfriend. He thrust his forearm at the wolf's muzzle saying: 'Tell him to bite on to me, Brat. I can hold him.'

Dragonfriend repeated the order in the Elder tongue and Drinks-the-Wind's huge jaws closed on the man's arm.

Dragonfriend let go the wolf's ruff and flung her body over the man's legs, shouting to the soldiers to help her weight him down. For a few terrifying minutes, the wolf hung motionless from the man's arm while belts and reins were hurriedly buckled together and woven to form a mesh long and strong enough to pull Drinks-the-Wind to safety. Three men held each end and the loop was swung carefully beneath the wolf's hindquarters and drawn up until his weight was on the leather.

Now the soldiers holding the man's legs began to pull him slowly backwards. The wolf still had his teeth in the man's arm but the men holding the mesh heaved... The wolf rose slowly.

Cricket was afraid he would struggle but he kept still and at last his hind legs were on the road bed once more.

Everyone stood up and began laughing and talking. Dragonfriend embraced the Overlord's man who had saved Drinks-the-Wind, hugged the wolf, wept a little, thanked the soldiers and the lord and returned to the edge of the broken span to call across to Cricket.

'Go with Stark to the next bridge down,' she shouted. 'I'll meet you there, but first I must make sure that Speedhand here visits a healer. You'll look after Cricket for me, won't you, Stark? If I'm not at the bridge, take him home with you and I'll come as soon as I can.'

Stark waved in reply and began to back her wagon off the bridge. There was not room to turn it until they reached the road. Everyone was buzzing with excitement but Cricket felt sicker and sicker until suddenly he lost his dinner behind a bush. Stark handed him a water bottle without comment.

'Tie your beasts on behind,' she told him, 'and ride with me. Now, I know you are called Cricket. What else is there to know?'

Very briefly, Cricket told her why he was travelling with Dragonfriend. To his amazement she knew about Gaingold.

'Who told you?' he asked. 'I thought the storytellers did not know about me till very recently.'

'They may not have known who you were or where you were but they knew Gaingold had turned down an apprentice storyteller vouched for by Storyteller Spring Rain,' said Stark. 'His story is being told all over the place. I heard it three days' journey to the east.'

She waved her whip vaguely to their left. 'You're quite famous, young feller-me-lad.'

Cricket sat quiet for some distance, trying to absorb this. He felt odd – not quite real – just as when Dragonfriend had told him how important the storytellers' Guild thought him.

Presently he said: 'Do you know the man who saved Drinks-the-Wind?'

Stark looked sharply at him. 'Speedhand? Yes, of course. He's the Young Swordsman.' She clicked her tongue at his blank expression.

'Sun save us, child, Speedhand is the finest swordsman in the Joined Lands and ought to be the Swordsman. He is too soft-hearted to challenge the man who holds the title at the moment, so he is only the Young Swordsman. No sense, that young man. Well, not much; still, at least he had the sense to put his left arm into the wolf's jaws, not his right!'

'It was a very brave thing to do. He saved Dragonfriend's life as well as Drinks-the-Wind's,' Cricket said, wishing that he could have been so heroic. 'I could never have held the wolf's weight, even if I had thought fast enough to do as Speedhand did.'

'You did all you could and better than some. It was you told them to use their belts,' Stark reminded him. She slapped him painfully on the back, almost knocking him off the driving seat.

When Cricket stopped coughing, he decided that she was right. He had done the best he could.

CHAPTER SIX

Stark drove the cart along to the next bridge.

A road had been hewn out of the rock along the side of the valley. It wound down to the valley's floor to join the greater road from the east. The bridge there had its drawbridge in constant use, and they had to wait for some time while a string of barges sailed slowly upstream under the raised drawbridge, helped on by men ashore pulling on ropes.

When at last they got across, Dragonfriend and Drinks-the-Wind were waiting for them.

Dragonfriend assured them that Speedhand was not much hurt. The Overlord's own Healer had examined the bite and cleaned it and bound it up.

'He's not to use it for a few days and has to rest for a while,' she told them. She looked round to see that nobody was near enough to hear, which with the wolf at her side was unlikely, and said softly, 'Stark, did you know how ill the Overlord is?'

Stark frowned. 'I knew he had taken to his bed but nothing more.'

'I believe he is dying,' whispered Dragonfriend. 'I saw him, just for a moment. He'd been asking for me, Healer Goldthread says, but he didn't know me.' She blinked and swallowed hard. 'And Graycat is away – there is some sort of trouble in the Seaward Hills and she had to go to settle it. Still, at least Farwalker is expected in the next day or two.'

Cricket had never imagined that he would be lodged in the Overlord's own dwelling, the Great House. But Dragonfriend had her own rooms there, close to the apartments of the Young Overlord and he was told that he might as well be using one of them.

'They do need airing,' said Dragonfriend, looking critically around the room with a determinedly housewifely air. She caught his eye and laughed. 'Well, so I'm told! Now, how would you like to meet some of my friends and have lastmeal with them? If you are not too tired for a short walk, that is.'

So she took him to meet the old blind Trader Gather and Medley, who was not only a Blademistress but also Gather's eyes. She was quite startlingly beautiful but Cricket thought he had never seen anyone so withdrawn. She would smile quietly at Dragonfriend but later, when Speedhand turned up, his arm in a sling, followed by Carter Stark, both of them slightly drunk and very cheerful, Medley sat silent and expressionless for a few minutes and then slipped away.

Dragonfriend scolded Speedhand for drinking when he was hurt. 'If you fall and open the wound, I shan't pity you,' she told him fiercely. 'It would serve you right.'

'Oh, let it go, Brat,' said Stark. 'I'm looking after him tonight. You're the one should have an early night, y'know. The storyteller has set the enquiry for tomorrow at the second hour after dawn.'

Dragonfriend caught her breath and looked anxiously at Cricket. He looked back, wondering.

Then he knew. 'Gaingold?' he asked her.

'Yes. Silkentongue must have summoned as many Storytellers as possible as soon as he heard we were on our way. I sent a message by pigeon before we left Edgescarp. An enquiry into a storyteller's integrity does not happen often, Cricket.'

'There has not been one in the Joined Lands for fifty years at least,' said Gather. 'And then it was nothing like so serious.'

Cricket felt curiously hollow; and found nothing to say.

Next morning he could not eat a mouthful. Dragonfriend, lavishly dribbling honey over her porridge, tried to distract him by speculating on the weird notions of those who refused to sweeten porridge.

'They must enjoy suffering,' she said, peering at him. 'I expect they cook their bread without salt, like the lady in the tale who told her father that she loved him as much as bread loves salt. Did you ever hear it? He thought she was mocking him and banished her from his land... Well, I'll tell it to you some other time. Do try to eat something, Cricket. I should think it will be most of the day before we get another meal.'

But Cricket couldn't. He shook his head, drank some milk and then wished he hadn't. It lay heavily in his belly. Dragonfriend made him put a chunk of bread in his pouch and they set off for the storytellers' Guildhall.

It was packed, and noisy. All the storytellers seemed to be talking and none of them listening. Dragonfriend was recognised at once and the two of them were passed forward to the front row of benches, where those already installed squeezed up to give them room.

Cricket stared up at the massive roof beams above and the pillars, which appeared to be whole tree trunks, holding them up, at the carved panels forming the walls and at the floor inlaid with symbols he did not recognise.

He looked round at the storytellers. Nearly all of them seemed to be looking at him. He hurriedly turned to gaze at his feet, feeling hotter and hotter and sure that everyone was laughing at his embarrassment. Then there was a sudden stir and silence fell as the Storyteller came quietly in by a small door at the front of the room.

He was short and slight and old and he looked very fragile. Cricket heard Dragonfriend catch her breath as her great-uncle moved carefully across to the high-backed chair set in the centre of the space facing them all.

He sat down and inclined his head to the gathering. Then he spoke and at once Cricket was bewitched. He had never heard such a voice; like honey for smoothness, clear and distinct as a golden bell, it fell on the ear like a caress. Yet all the Storyteller actually said was: 'This enquiry will now begin.'

He paused and looked round at all of them. 'Let no one think that this has been lightly undertaken. The guildmasters have been long in consultation, we have heard witnesses and we have considered many aspects of this case. Our duty as guild members is inescapable: there must be an inquiry and it must be witnessed by as many members of the Guild of Storytellers as possible. That said, let there be no more delay.

'Gaingold Storyteller stands charged with deliberate deceit in his capacity of Storyteller in that he led the boy, Cricket Broadleaf's son, to believe that he was not acceptable to this guild. This he did knowing that Storyteller Spring Rain had vouched for the boy and had promised him her help.

'Storyteller Spring Rain herself was unable to travel. She sent a message to Gaingold by the mouth of Thornbeard Storyteller, who is here present and will speak for himself. Thornbeard?'

A stocky young man with a truly remarkable black beard sprouting eagerly in all directions stepped forward.

'A little over a year ago,' he began, 'I was on my way to the Scarp district and I passed through Brownhill. Naturally, I stopped to pay my respects to Storyteller Spring Rain. She begged me to try to catch Gaingold Storyteller before he began his round of the Scarp villages, to tell him that there was a lad in the village of Edgescarp who would make a Storyteller. She said that she had promised the lad that she would take him as an apprentice and it was very much on her mind that she could not fulfil her promise.

'I offered to go to the village myself; but Rain thought that Gaingold might be hurt to be bypassed so.

'"It is his right," she said to me. "It is not so often that we find new blood; let him have the joy of it." So I sought out Gaingold when I reached the Scarp and gave him the message. If he did not want to take the lad on himself, he was to send him to Brownhill and Spring Rain would arrange for his apprenticeship. There was no suggestion,' and Thornbeard's voice slowed a little, 'not the smallest suggestion that Gaingold should judge the boy himself. Spring Rain had no thought but that her Cricket was worthy.'

Cricket found he was blinking back tears. It was so like Storyteller Rain. He promised himself that no matter what happened at this inquiry, he would somehow get to Brownhill and see Rain to thank her.

'Does anyone wish to question Thornbeard Storyteller?' asked Silkentongue. He waited, but there was no reply. There was utter silence. Cricket was holding his breath.

'There can therefore be no doubt,' Silkentongue went on, 'that Gaingold Storyteller knew Storyteller Spring Rain's intention. He knew her and he knew her reputation. He must have known that she would not make such a recommendation unless she was sure that the lad would indeed make a storyteller.

'There is still the possibility of misunderstanding on the boy's part. We must look at this very carefully, guildmembers, for the honour of us all is at stake.'

There was a murmur round the great room and Dragonfriend nudged Cricket gently.

The Storyteller shifted uneasily in his padded chair. He looked tired and ill and Cricket wondered how he could bear this crowd and heat.

'Cricket, Broadleaf's son,' said the Storyteller and the boy jerked to attention.

CHAPTER SEVEN

'Cricket, please stand here,' said the Storyteller softly. His voice was so warm and soothing to the ear that Cricket almost missed his meaning. Then he scrambled forward nervously to stand beside him.

'Did Gaingold Storyteller ever tell you that you could not become an apprentice storyteller?' asked Silkentongue.

'Why, of course he –' Cricket stopped and corrected himself. 'No, not in so many words,' he said cautiously.

'What did he say?'

Cricket gulped. 'He said: 'A storyteller? You? Skies forbid!' and – and sniggered.' He reproduced the sneering tone exactly; it had echoed in his memory long enough. 'And then he said that Storyteller Spring Rain must have been in her dotage to suggest it. Half the village heard him,' Cricket added, as unemotionally as he could.

'What did you and your family understand by this?'

'That I had been rejected.'

'But it was never actually so stated?'

'No.' Despairingly, Cricket thought that Gaingold was going to win, after all. For indeed he had not lied, not really. *And I,* thought Cricket, *shall still owe him a year of misery.* He set his teeth and waited to hear Gaingold acquitted. But they had not yet finished with him.

'Why did you not press Gaingold Storyteller for his reasons if you thought you were unfairly rejected?' asked a brisk middle aged woman.

'He was on the point of leaving and –' Cricket stopped, remembering far too well his choking disappointment. He swallowed and went on, carefully controlling his voice: 'and I was numb with despair. I did not seem able to think.'

'Did you ever consider appealing, later on?'

He shook his head. 'No. To whom could we appeal?'

'So you and all your people took it for granted that his word, his judgement, was final,' she summed up.

Cricket could not detect any scorn in her tone, but surely she must feel it. He nodded, dumbly.

'Cricket Storyteller,' the Storyteller leaned forward and Cricket turned to him, grateful for the title. 'How do you feel now towards Gaingold Storyteller?'

The boy thought it over. Dragonfriend had warned him to be tactful and keep his temper but he was tired of being careful. They wanted to know what he felt? Very well, he'd tell them.

Cricket tilted his head and filled his lungs as Dragonfriend had taught him.

'Just about the way I'd feel towards a cockroach I found in my dinner,' he said, very distinctly. And thought, *Now I'm in for it! I've thrown it all away.* Stars, but it was satisfying!

But when he looked around he saw broad grins on most faces and the Storyteller himself had a hand over his mouth, coughing. His face was perfectly straight, however, when he lowered his hand.

'Gaingold Storyteller, how say you to this witness?' he asked, and Gaingold rose and strode forward to glare at the boy.

'I say that this peasant brat is a fool,' he said. He sounded confident and he relaxed his glare to smile round at his audience.

Cricket saw Dragonfriend sit up alertly as if something had caught her attention but everyone else waited quietly to hear Gaingold out.

'I suppose if stupidity had become a qualification for a Storyteller I should have been told,' he went on. 'For a clodhopper I suppose it hardly matters, but we Storytellers must have our wits about us. I see nothing wrong in suppressing unrealistic pretensions.'

Cricket recalled Dragonfriend saying at their evening fire, 'If someone suddenly starts using long words, he may just be pompous or he may be nervous. Fear takes different people differently.'

Gaingold was not as sure of himself as he wanted folk to think. Cricket's stomach began to untwist.

Then Dragonfriend raised a hand and the Storyteller nodded to her. She stood up in her place.

'Guildmembers, does anyone object if I give this gathering an example of Cricket's intelligence?' she asked politely.

Silkentongue looked at Gaingold, waited a moment to let him protest if he wished then, as Gaingold stood scowlingly silent, he nodded. 'That seems reasonable. You have leave.'

Dragonfriend gave Cricket a quick smile and began: 'As you will all have heard, the High Bridge lost its wooden span while Cricket and I were crossing it yesterday. My wolf friend Drinks-the-Wind saved my life by thrusting me onto the safe portion; but he himself was left hanging over the drop, in very grave danger. Cricket could not help physically because he was on the far side of the bridge.

'But he was the only person quick-witted enough to see how Drinks-the-Wind might be saved. He shouted across the gap to those on my side to use their belts and reins to pull the wolf up.'

Gaingold interrupted sharply, 'I thought it was your noble ex-bandit friend who saved the wolf. Didn't he put on a great show of self sacrifice, shoving his arm into the creature's mouth?'

Dragonfriend tilted her head very slightly in his direction. She did not look at him but kept her eyes on Silkentongue. 'Yes, if it had not been for Speedhand, I could not have held my cousin wolf until the men had completed their sling. But if Cricket had not so quickly told them what to do, the sling would never have been ready in time.'

Gaingold was no longer lounging at his ease. He drew himself up and stared hatefully at Dragonfriend; then he turned his glare on the boy. Cricket felt his scalp tighten as he clenched his teeth and stared back. If he had been a wolf, his ears would have been flat to his skull and the hair along his spine standing up in bristles. As it was, he found he wanted to bare his teeth.

The Storyteller's dispassionate voice broke in on them. 'Will you now agree, Gaingold, that you were mistaken in your estimate of this boy's wits? And in your judgement of Spring Rain's?'

Gaingold switched his glare to Silkentongue.

'What does that senile old woman know about standards?' he demanded vindictively. He swung back to the assembled Storytellers. 'How shall we earn even a bare living if any ignorant cub is allowed to undercut us? We should be closing our ranks, not allowing nobodies from other guilds to join us! Look at the actors! They steal our audiences; they should be put down! But oh, no! One of the Storyteller's grandchildren is a playactor –' he almost spat the word out in disgust, 'so nothing is done. How shall we do when we have no more influence, no power, no listeners, when clods like this boy –' his voice rose almost to a shriek, 'drag us down, destroy our reputations, ruin our market...'

'That is enough!' The Storyteller's voice was steely cold as he cut across Gaingold's frantic ranting. Gaingold stopped dead and stood panting and staring wildly around. Silkentongue went on levelly: 'You have condemned yourself out of your own mouth, Gaingold.'

He looked along the rows of men, women and children, all Storytellers, Masters, journeymen or apprentices, all shocked and bursting to speak. A buzz was rising. His look silenced it.

'Does anyone here disagree with me?'

No one spoke.

Into this silence Silkentongue, the Storyteller of the Joined Lands, the Overlord's Court Storyteller, passed sentence.

'Gaingold,' he said slowly and heavily, 'you are no longer a Storyteller. You shall never tell another story as long as you live. You have heard that title for the last time.'

Gaingold's hands rose to his face; he held one to his mouth and the other palm out before his eyes, as if to ward off the terrible words.

'You have brought shame upon your guild and upon your family and upon your Name. Therefore you shall no more be called Gaingold. You hear that name now for the last time. Instead, for what you have done to all storytellers everywhere, since Truth distorted is worse than a lie outright, you shall have another Name.'

His voice grew even colder.

'I Name you Gainscorn.'

He brought the flat of his hand sharply down on the broad arm of his chair.

The crack of it seemed to bring Gainscorn out of his paralysis.

'No!' he screamed. 'No, no, no!! I am Storyteller born – you can't take my birthright from me – you can't!

'You!' He flung round on Cricket, panting. 'You are no Storyteller. Born of mud, how dare you tell tales of your betters! And you, forsworn, name-lost,' he lurched towards Dragonfriend, 'because you are kin to that self-righteous shut-mind there, you think you can get away with any lies!'

He spat the words at her with his face thrust almost into hers but Dragonfriend did not move a muscle.

Some of the younger men nearby took hold of Gainscorn and drew him away, quite gently but firmly. He struggled and writhed, weeping, howling curses at them, at Silkentongue, at Dragonfriend and at the whole Guild of Storytellers until he was man-handled out of the room.

Cricket was shaking so hard that he had to hold onto Silkentongue's chair. He found that he was actually weeping and let go to mop his cheeks hastily on his sleeve, ashamed to be seen crying like a baby in this company.

Then he saw that the Storyteller was weeping, too. Cricket leaned forward to shield him from the rest of the storytellers and he clutched the boy's arm.

'Help me up, Cricket,' he said softly. 'Oh, Sky and Stars! I never thought to have to do that. I would that I had died sooner.'

He sounded so despairing that Cricket longed to comfort him; but what comfort could there be? He got the Storyteller to his feet and the old man, suddenly so much older, straightened himself and walked steadily to the door.

The storytellers gave way respectfully before him.

'That was well done of you, Cricket Storyteller,' said Dragonfriend into his ear. 'Sweetvoice, his wife, will take care of him now. Suppose we slip away as quietly as we can. I do not feel like being congratulated just now, do you?'

Cricket agreed fervently.

CHAPTER EIGHT

Outside, the street was crowded with storytellers all talking at once about the dreadful sentence that Silkentongue had passed on Gainscorn. Nobody thought it unjust but there was a feeling that the Storyteller should not have had to do it.

'It will kill him,' said one man fussily. 'Surely it could have been dealt with quietly somehow?'

'Don't be more of an idiot than you can help, my dear,' drawled a slender elegant woman. 'Once Silkentongue got hold of the story it could not be hushed up. He would never allow it.'

'Who said anything about hushing it up?' The fussy man, surprisingly, did not seem to mind being called an idiot but was upset by this.

Dragonfriend pulled Cricket into a doorway to let them pass.

'We don't need that pair telling us how we should have behaved,' she said, screwing up her nose in distaste. 'That was Shellgather and his sister. He is a stickler for accuracy and she'll twist his words unmercifully to tease him, but once they get started on someone outside the family, well, you have to gag them to stop them.'

'Unlike you, Brat?' said a man's voice behind us.

Dragonfriend swung round, amazed and delighted. 'Farwalker!' she gasped.

Cricket was surprised. From what Dragonfriend had told of Farwalker, he had expected someone startling, but Farwalker, the Archer of the Joined Lands, was a very ordinary looking man. He was not tall, although he had the very broad well-muscled shoulders and arms of a bowman, of course. His face was not ugly, or even plain, just – well, ordinary. You could have found his dark brown hair, brown skin and brown eyes anywhere in the Joined Lands. In Edgescarp, even.

Then Cricket looked again and saw more. Farwalker had an air of complete self-possession and authority. Cricket felt very small and unimportant again.

Dragonfriend gave him a further surprise. He had expected her to fling her arms around Farwalker, hail him as Baylock and chatter about all that had happened since she last saw him but she greeted him almost with formality and was so subdued that Farwalker asked her if she were ill.

'No, just tired,' she told him, smiling uncertainly. 'When did you get back?'

'About an hour ago. We heard last night of your little excitement on the bridge. I decided that if you are going to get into trouble again, it might be a good idea to be around. So we set out at dawn. I had to report to the Overlord before I could come and find you, though.'

'You must be much more tired than I am, if you've been riding since dawn. How did you find the Overlord?'

Farwalker shook his head. 'He was like a man in a dream. I think he recognised me for a moment but... Healer Goldthread says that he can't last much longer. And Gray not here!'

'Suppose the trouble in the Seaward Hills was set on purpose to draw her out of reach at his death?' suggested Dragonfriend, frowning anxiously.

Farwalker shook his head. 'No, that has been on the simmer for some while. It has merely come to a boil,' he said. 'Now, tell me how the trial went.'

Dragonfriend told him, very briefly and he frowned.

'What will happen to Gainscorn now?' he asked.

Dragonfriend shrugged. 'He will have to find some work, I suppose. He still has a Name, of sorts. And he did gain a good deal of gold. He can live on it for a while. In his place, I'd leave the country as soon as I could.'

'Would you? But you are not Gainscorn. He may prefer to stay and take revenge. I think I shall escort you and Cricket back to the Great House,' said Farwalker, seriously.

Dragonfriend said solemnly, 'I am always glad of your company, my lord,' and laughed aloud at his disgusted expression. 'No, I don't believe Gainscorn will try to attack either me or Cricket but if you want to escort us, of course you are welcome. You are always welcome, Farwalker,' and she suddenly hugged him, just as Cricket had expected her to do when they met.

They returned to the Great House talking cheerfully together, Dragonfriend making sure that Cricket was included in the conversation. At the side door which Dragonfriend generally used however, they were brought to a startled halt.

A small, very thin girl in a ragged tunic and trews waited there, hopping agitatedly from one foot to the other. As soon as she saw them, she pounced upon Dragonfriend.

'Strongtower sent me to warn you but the guards couldn't tell me where you were. He says there is danger threatening the Overlord and the Corulli Ambassador is mixed up in it somehow, but he doesn't know any more,' she gabbled, without once pausing for breath.

'Strongtower should have sent to Lord Buckler,' began Farwalker, but Dragonfriend shook her head.

'Never mind that now. We must go at once to the Overlord.'

'When I left him, I was told no one was to see him. We shan't be admitted.'

'You forget: I have the Right of Immediate Audience,' Dragonfriend told him. 'I have never needed to use it before but I think now is the time.'

'Come then.' Lord Farwalker led them through the long hallways at a pace which was only just short of a run.

Dragonfriend and Cricket had to trot to keep up. Servants, courtiers and the occasional guard looked after them, amused or startled or disapproving but no one stopped or questioned them until they reached the Overlord's chamber.

There the two guards at the door stepped forward.

'No one may disturb the Overlord,' said one of them. 'The Corulli Ambassador is with him.'

Dragonfriend, trying not to pant, said in a controlled voice: 'I am Storyteller Wolftalker Dragonfriend. I have the Right of Immediate Audience which I now invoke. Stand aside.'

The first guard made a move to the door but the other stopped her. He smiled unpleasantly at Dragonfriend and said, 'Ah, but it was Storyteller Spellbinder who was given the right, wasn't it? So we can't...'

He stopped on that word. Farwalker's hand was at his throat.

'Guardsman,' said Farwalker, very softly, in a tone that made Cricket's back hair prickle, 'the Right was given to Brook Weaveword's daughter, before ever she was Named Spellbinder. Now, have you any further remarks to make about Names? If not, the Young Overlord's Storyteller shall exercise her undoubted Right, the granting of which I, personally, witnessed.'

The woman guard waited no longer. Ignoring her half-choked fellow, she thrust open the door.

'Storyteller Wolftalker Dragonfriend claims her Right of Immediate Audience!' she announced.

Cricket peered over Dragonfriend's shoulder. The room was very dim for the curtains were drawn almost together. Mere cracks of light spilled onto the floor and outlined the man bending over the propped up form of the Overlord. He straightened himself and stepped forward as if to bar their entrance.

But Dragonfriend and Cricket were already in the bedchamber and Farwalker, still holding the guard by the throat, dragged him in after them.

The woman guard, following, exclaimed, 'But where is Healer Goldthread? He went in a quarter hour ago and has not come out yet!'

'The healer retired into the inner chamber to prepare a

draught,' said the Ambassador quickly, in a curiously muffled voice. 'What does this unseemly intrusion mean?'

Dragonfriend had seemed to shrink within herself at the guardsman's jibe. Now she revived. She walked briskly over to a door at the far side of the room, saying over her shoulder, 'It means that I wish to have audience of the Overlord. Shall we leave it to his healer to decide...?'

The Ambassador made as if to go after her. 'Leave that door alone!' he ordered. 'Goldthread wants to work undisturbed!'

Farwalker picked up the guardsman bodily and threw him across the Ambassador's path.

If Cricket had not seen it for himself, he would not have believed it possible. The guard was a tall man and broad with it, yet Farwalker treated him like a toy. The Ambassador fell, tangled with the unfortunate guard, and Dragonfriend flung open the inner door.

She exclaimed in horror and Cricket ran to peer over her shoulder. The healer lay crumpled on the floor, quite still.

Dragonfriend knelt to feel his pulse and sighed in relief.

'He is alive,' she said. 'What did you do, hit him on the head?' and she glared furiously at the Ambassador, who was still getting to his feet.

Behind them the woman guard said: 'A healer! Someone must fetch the Young Overlord's healer. I know Healer Ayegreen is somewhere in the Great House today but I may not leave my post. Will you seek her, Storyteller?'

'With all my heart,' agreed Dragonfriend at once. 'I'll send some more guards, too. Is that man armed?'

Both guards were shocked.

'Of course not!' exclaimed the woman. 'No one bears arms in the Overlord's House.'

'So you did not search him, then,' said Farwalker, grimly. He had the Ambassador by the shoulder and jerked the man into one of the shafts of light leaking between the curtains.

Dragonfriend stopped dead on her way to the door. 'That is not the Corulli Ambassador!' she gasped. 'I know the Ambassador; so do you, Farwalker. This is an imposter!'

Farwalker turned the man's face to the light.

'You're right, Brat,' he agreed. 'But how did he get past the guards?'

'I swear, as my name is Russet Warrior, that it was the Ambassador who entered this room!' cried the woman guard. 'He did not look like this man then. How has he changed? Sorcery!' and she backed away, making the sign against witchcraft.

'No,' said Dragonfriend suddenly, 'not sorcery. Hypnotism! I've seen one in such a sleep as Goldthread's before, now I think of it. Don't look this man in the face; better gag him as well.'

She turned to the door again. 'I'll go seek Ayegreen and other help.' She was gone, running fast along the passage.

Farwalker and Russet hastily gagged and bound their prisoner. Cricket went over to the Overlord's bed, wondering how he had slept through all the commotion, only to be pulled away by the other guard.

'No one goes near my Lord,' he said in a hoarse whisper. 'I've failed him once, letting in that creature...' He could not go on.

Cricket said quickly, 'But it was not your fault. He made you and Russet think he was the Ambassador. You had no reason to deny him entrance or to suspect him.'

He shook his head. 'Who knows what he may have done to my Lord? My blame!'

'Don't try to talk,' Cricket urged him. It was obviously painful for him. He added, for courtesy, 'I am called Cricket Storyteller.'

'Safebide Borderer,' he returned; and his face twisted in misery. 'Shall lose that Name now,' he whispered. He put out a hand and laid it very softly over the Overlord's, limp on the bedcover.

Cricket could see that he loved his Lord. Indeed, he seemed a different man now from the one who had flung that cruel jibe at

Dragonfriend. Could the hypnotist have somehow forced him to be cruel? Russet had been surprised at his sneer. Perhaps the prisoner had simply instructed him to keep everyone out by any means possible. Cricket made up his mind to ask a healer if this could be so, as soon as he had a chance.

Help began to arrive. Four guards, two to relieve Russet and Safebide, two to remove the prisoner; then their captain; then a very young and nervous apprentice healer, Yarrow, who became miraculously calm as soon as he reached the Overlord.

Shortly after came Lord Buckler, the Overlord's Trustman, very stern and self-controlled; several courtiers; a tiny elderly lady with very bright black eyes who greeted Farwalker familiarly and at once took brisk charge of everyone; and finally, Healer Ayegreen and a breathless Dragonfriend.

'Lady Jewel,' said the healer, looking round the room which, large though it was, had become quite crowded, 'will you have the room cleared, please,' and in seconds most people were leaving. The little lady was very forceful.

'I shall want to talk to the two guards who may have been hypnotised,' said Ayegreen, 'and you must stay, Yarrow Healer, of course.'

Yarrow at once became clumsy with embarrassment. The last Cricket saw of him as they left, he was picking up the contents of a small chest of jewels that he had knocked flying. He dropped quite half of those he picked up.

'He'll be all right,' said Lord Farwalker, catching Cricket's glance. 'All he needs is someone who needs him.'

CHAPTER NINE

Lord Farwalker halted just outside the door of the Overlord's apartments and looked around. He beckoned to the guards-captain who was hesitating in the corridor.

'You should post more guards here, Captain, as backup for the two on the door. Suppose you have some in this side corridor, within sight of the door but unobtrusive. If anything happened to the regular guards, they'd see and be able to come to their help.'

The captain agreed at once, his gloomy expression lightening somewhat. Farwalker smiled at him.

'Cheer up, man,' he said. 'No one blames you for not foreseeing the unforeseeable. None of us ever thought that our Overlord could be in any danger.'

'Yes,' murmured Dragonfriend in Cricket's ear, 'the guard has been purely ceremonial for years. Even when Westfold invaded, the Overlord's guard bore no weapons. Now the unthinkable has happened.'

She looked sadly at the Overlord's closed door. They both started as Lady Jewel suddenly appeared at Farwalker's elbow.

'And now I shall call a meeting of the Overlord's council,' stated the Lady. 'Dragonfriend, you and your apprentice must attend; and you, Lord Farwalker. Now, which of the councillors will be in the City at present?'

'Can you call a council meeting on your own, Lady?' asked Farwalker as they all moved off.

'It is legal,' announced Jewel. 'And there is precedent. Tell us, Remembrancer.'

Dragonfriend jerked to attention. 'Precedent. Yes. When

Overlord Makepeace was thrown from his horse and lay stunned for seven days, he having as yet no Young Overlord to call the council together, a member of that council called a meeting. The councillors made decisions in the Overlord's name until he recovered. That was in the year...'

'No matter for the year,' interrupted Jewel, briskly. 'Page! I want all the messengers you can round up in the council chamber in five minutes. Run!'

The page made a hasty bow and vanished.

'Let me see,' murmured Jewel, pausing and tapping her fingernails against her teeth. 'Deepskill. Is she still in the City? And...' She began counting off the lords and ladies who must be summoned and Cricket realised from the intent expression on Dragonfriend's face that she was memorising these names and that he should be doing so also. He barely noticed when they reached the council chamber, so absorbed had he become.

The first act of the council was to send a Hand of guardsmen to the Seaward Hills to tell the Young Overlord what had happened. Then Healer Ayegreen came to report to them that the Overlord did not appear to have been harmed. But she would not take the risk of trying to bring him back to consciousness, saying that his sleep was doing him good, whether it was natural or not. She had examined Healer Goldthread and decided to leave him to sleep also. Yarrow Healer was watching him and the Overlord for any signs of stirring while Ayegreen reported to the council.

'I am satisfied that the two guards were indeed hypnotised,' she said firmly. 'The man who did it was a master, so speedily and smoothly were they convinced. Both Safebide and Russet still feel sure that they allowed the Ambassador to pass them, even though they know it was really the prisoner. As I say, a Master Hypnotist.'

'How can this attack have profited the hypnotist?' asked Jewel. 'Have you any way to find out?'

Ayegreen said quickly, 'Not by questioning the prisoner! Perhaps another hypnotist could deal with him but I cannot. It may be possible to question the Overlord and Healer Goldthread when they awake, by putting them under further hypnotism. I am no expert in this and I would not undertake it myself; but I fear what Healer Goldthread may have been instructed by the prisoner to do. I do not think he should be allowed to come near the Overlord until we know more.'

There was an uncomfortable silence as the councillors considered her words.

Then Lady Deepskill said: 'Who is the best hypnotist in the Joined Lands?'

'To my knowledge, Healer Agrimony. He has already been sent for,' said Ayegreen. 'I wished for his advice whatever your lordships' decision might be.'

Her gaze was steady on Lady Deepskill and she paid no heed to a grumble from an anxious councillor about the danger of taking decisions without consultation.

Lord Buckler broke in impatiently. 'We must know what is behind this attack and debating will get us nowhere.' He stood up decisively and bowed to the council. 'By your leaves, my place is beside the Overlord. I am still his Trustman, however misplaced that trust on this occasion. I can bear this talk no longer! Come, Healer. My apologies, councillors,' and he made his way clumsily to the door. Ayegreen waited a moment, then bowed and followed him.

Cricket glimpsed Lord Buckler's face as he turned from the council. It was twisted in misery. Cricket had felt sorry for Safebide; he felt sorrier still for the Trustman, and looked away quickly.

Lady Jewel watched Lord Buckler go and shook her head sadly. 'We are all tired. Let us bring this council to an end now,' she said. 'Remembrancer Dragonfriend, will you and your apprentice please stay in your rooms that we may be sure of your safety. Your evidence may be important.'

'I shall stay with them,' said Farwalker abruptly. He was looking strained and tired. 'They may need a guard.'

Jewel considered this. 'I think the two guards, Russet and Safebide had better do that,' she said. 'Who else will be more aware of the danger? And I shall need you, my lord, to help organise defences, if defences we must have.'

So they found themselves more or less prisoners in Dragonfriend's rooms until the Young Overlord should return. Drinks-the-Wind hated it and Cricket did not like it at all. Russet and Safebide took turns to rest and allowed no one to enter, not even Speedhand who offered to share the duty with them. They refused.

Dragonfriend claimed to be glad of the chance to rest but was soon busy telling Cricket stories, making him learn more of the Elder tongue and coaxing their life histories out of Safebide and Russet.

But even she was relieved when a great bustle on the third day announced cat's arrival. 'Now we'll get out of here,' she said eagerly.

Graycat swept into the room, saying over her shoulder: 'I shall do it myself. Attend me in the council chamber.'

She turned to Dragonfriend who was bowing low, caught her hands and drew her up to kiss her on the cheek.

'My best thanks for saving the Overlord from Dreamtalker, Brat. I have already told Farwalker of my gratitude,' she said warmly.

'Now,' she went on briskly, 'There is no need for you to stay here anymore. The hypnotist Dreamtalker has been questioned by Healer Agrimony and is safely locked up, Healer Goldthread is unharmed and back with the Overlord, who is in no worse health than he was before. The difficulty is that we still do not know what, if anything, Dreamtalker told the Overlord to do. Agrimony could not make Dreamtalker speak about it and the Overlord is not well enough to be questioned.'

She stopped her rapid summing up and smiled at Cricket. 'You must be Cricket. Welcome, and forgive me for not greeting you at once.'

He would have forgiven her much more than that. The Young Overlord was like a strong wind which left you battered but invigorated and laughing.

He bowed and stammered something about being honoured and then Graycat swept them all out of the room, only stopping to speak to Safebide and Russet.

'You have been standing watch and watch, haven't you?' she said. 'You must be worn out. Take two whole days' leave before you return to the Overlord's guard. Yes, of course you are to return. The Overlord will be safer with you to guard him than if I stood watch myself. Or Drinks-the-Wind, here!' and she laughed and patted the wolf who accepted the attention calmly.

They were whisked along to the council chamber where Graycat dealt rapidly with all the business of the Land which had been awaiting her, gave her formal approval to the council's actions and then announced her intention of interviewing the hypnotist, Dreamtalker. At once all the councillors protested. Only Farwalker, who was present by Graycat's order although not a member of the council, said nothing. He grinned across at Dragonfriend, spread his hands and shrugged. 'What else would she do?' his expression said.

Dreamtalker was well guarded but the guards were stationed out of sight of their prisoner and were watched in their turn by a second set of guards at the far end of the passage, out of earshot of him. In this way he could not, it was hoped, catch them in the spell of his eye and voice.

Graycat told Agrimony, an incredibly old and frail little man, to wait with the second set of guards, Farwalker to stay with the nearer ones and Dragonfriend to keep beside her as witness.

'You stay with Lord Farwalker, Cricket,' she said; then, as his face fell, 'Oh, very well, you may come too, if you wish.'

The prisoner rose as they came up to his cell. The door was all of bars so that they could see him and every corner of the cell. He was quite comfortably housed. He had a bed, a chair and a small table and several candles to light him. He stood very still, staring at them and Cricket wanted to shut his eyes and stop his ears. He was scared. Could the man cast his spell over them even when they were all on guard against him?

Graycat said: 'You are Dreamtalker. I am Graycat. I wish to know what commands you have set upon my great uncle. If you tell me the truth, you shall go free and unharmed.'

Dreamtalker looked startled at her frankness. Then he said slowly, 'How can I believe you? And how can you believe me?'

'We can check what you say. Healer Agrimony tells me that he can rouse the Overlord and ask him if what you say is true. This will not harm him as would trying to find out from him what you told him to do,' replied Graycat. 'As for your believing me, I am the Young Overlord.'

Dreamtalker snorted. 'Lords! They give their word and take it back again as it suits them,' he said scornfully.

Cricket swallowed hard, expecting Graycat to be furious with him but she was unmoved.

'Perhaps you will believe my Storyteller,' she said calmly.

Dreamtalker's angry glare turned on Dragonfriend. She said firmly, 'I will back the Young Overlord's word with my own Name and the Guild of Storytellers will confirm it. My apprentice, Cricket Storyteller is my witness.'

Dreamtalker peered at her. 'You are Storyteller Wolftalker Dragonfriend,' he said. 'Some might say that your word is not worth much, Spellbinder-that-was. I, however, would say that it is better than the word of any other in the whole of the Joined Lands. Nevertheless, I do not take it. I was paid to do as I did and I gave my word to do it and keep silent.'

With that he turned his back on them and would say no more.

'An honest man!' Graycat gazed thoughtfully at the back of

his head. 'Sir, should you change your mind, ask the guards to send for me. I will come at any time.'

She turned away and they all followed her back to where Agrimony waited. Lord Farwalker joined them.

'You could try somewhat stronger persuasion,' he remarked lightly. Dragonfriend shuddered and Cricket felt cold all down his spine as he realised what he meant. Surely Graycat would not agree to torture?

'No.' Graycat did not change expression but Farwalker smiled at her.

'As you say,' he said. 'Well, Healer, what can you suggest?'

Healer Agrimony peered up at the Young Overlord. 'I would prefer not to question the Overlord. He is very weak and confused. There must, however, be something – some word or phrase that will unlock the memory.' He shook his head. 'It is a very long chance but I mean to try out whatever words occur to me and observe the effect. I fear it is of no use to attempt Dreamtalker's resolution again.'

'Try the words 'riot' and 'uprising',' said Farwalker grimly. He spoke softly, too low for the guards to hear.

Graycat turned to him sharply. 'Do you indeed think so?'

'And there is worse. I spoke with Strongtower only this morning. There are rumours that...' he broke off, looking at the guards and motioned Graycat away, along the passage.

'This is for your ears only, Young Overlord,' he said, suddenly formal.

'And my Remembrancer?'

Farwalker hesitated. 'Yes, I think she knows enough already,' he said reluctantly.

Graycat turned to them all. 'The guards are to remain here until relieved. If Dreamtalker asks for me, I am to be summoned no matter what the time of day or night. Healer, will you return to the Overlord and take Cricket with you? He can act as your witness and Remembrancer should the Overlord respond to you. I shall be in my private rooms.'

She went rapidly away with Lord Farwalker; and Dragonfriend followed, half running to keep up.

CHAPTER TEN

Cricket felt lost for the moment. He had hardly been out of Dragonfriend's company since they left Edgescarp. What was he supposed to do now? Then the healer tapped his shoulder.

'Come, young storyteller, we have work to do,' he said.

Healer Goldthread frowned at Cricket as they entered the Overlord's bedroom.

'What is that boy doing here?' he demanded. 'This is no place for children.'

'Ah, you have not met Cricket Storyteller,' said Agrimony, grinning wickedly. 'You were asleep when he last saw you. He is here as my witness and remembrancer, in case the Overlord should react to anything we say.'

Goldthread drew himself up. He was an imposing man, tall and stately, with a sharp nose and close cropped hair. He looked down at Cricket, his bushy eyebrows drawn together. Cricket bowed as respectfully as he could.

'The Young Overlord told me to be Healer Agrimony's witness, sir,' he said humbly.

Healer Goldthread snorted. The man who had been sitting silent by the bed looked round. It was Lord Buckler. Had he been sitting there ever since the council meeting?

'Graycat knows what she is about, Healer,' he said in a draggingly tired voice. 'The lad will behave himself.'

Cricket bowed much lower and said, 'Thank you, my lord.'

Agrimony, ignoring them all, had gone quietly over to the bed. He sighed, then said in a surprisingly loud firm voice, 'My Lord Strongmind!'

Cricket started. Until this moment he had never heard the Overlord's Name; he had ruled for so long, been simply The Overlord for so many years, that his personal name had been all but forgotten by most people. Now he stirred and his eyes opened slightly. Goldthread and Cricket moved nearer. Cricket was holding his breath and he suspected that Goldthread was, too.

Agrimony said, 'There are riots in some of the towns.'

He emphasised the word 'riot' slightly. The Overlord frowned; then his eyelids began to droop again. 'And an uprising in the Seaward Hills,' added the little healer.

The Overlord did not respond.

Agrimony looked at Goldthread and shrugged. He tried several other different ways of putting it, but the Overlord merely turned his head restlessly and spoke no word.

At last Agrimony left him to rest.

'In my opinion the man Dreamtalker did not have time to give my lord any instructions,' Goldthread told him. 'All this is a waste of time and not at all good for the Overlord. I would forbid it but that...'

'But that you might be wrong, hey?' Agrimony gave his wrinkled grin. 'Well, young storyteller, what do you think? What did you make of the hypnotist?'

Cricket pulled his thoughts together hurriedly. 'He certainly made me believe he had told the Overlord to do something. He is an impressive man,' he added, wondering how Lord Buckler would take this, 'and I think he is – well, too proud to lie. Graycat – the Young Overlord, I mean – said he was honest.'

'You think her judgement is to be relied on?' asked Agrimony, glancing slyly at him.

Cricket was shocked. 'It is not for me to pass any opinion on the Young Overlord,' he said. To his surprise, he found himself adding warmly: 'But I would risk my Name and my life on her judgement!' and knew it was true.

Goldthread drummed his fingers irritably on the window sill. 'This is getting us nowhere!' He turned sharply on Agrimony.

'Healer, I respect your years and your learning...'

'But?' Agrimony cocked his head enquiringly.

'Yes, BUT! I am in charge here. The Overlord's health is my responsibility and he is failing visibly. Nothing I can do will cure him; of that I am certain. All I can do now is ease his dying. I do not relish seeing him prodded and poked on the off chance...' he broke off and turned away to stride up and down the room in distress.

Lord Buckler rose and walked with him, speaking very softly; perhaps to comfort him.

Cricket looked anxiously at Healer Agrimony. He patted Cricket on the shoulder and asked him in a peaceful voice about the life of a storyteller and what Cricket should be doing as soon as Dragonfriend was free to continue his training.

They moved out of Goldthread's way, nearer to the great bed, as Cricket told him how he needed coaching in the Elder tongue and how Dragonfriend planned to take him to live with the Wilders, where he would be obliged to speak it all the time.

'And I'm longing to see the gildentrees,' he said, eagerly, almost forgetting his surroundings.

And at that moment the Overlord suddenly cried out, sitting bolt upright and glaring around him.

'No!' he exclaimed hoarsely, forcing the word out with immense effort. 'By the Stars, NO!' and he fell back, his head rolling limply to one side.

Both healers and his Trustman rushed to him. Cricket jumped back out of the way, appalled, wondering what he ought to do. Then Lord Buckler snapped over his shoulder: 'Send a guard for Graycat, at once!' and Cricket ran to the door and wrenched it open, calling to the guards outside.

The Young Overlord came running, Lord Farwalker at her shoulder and a very breathless Dragonfriend behind. Lady Jewel appeared shortly afterwards followed by other members of the council, courtiers, guards and servants.

Only the Young Overlord and her Remembrancer were let in. Cricket was allowed to stay and he huddled himself into a corner while Graycat bent over the bed and spoke softly to the healers.

Dragonfriend stayed close to her. Cricket was shivering and, for the first time since he had left home, wished himself back.

In a little while Lord Buckler, rising from where he had knelt beside the bed, said: 'He is dead.'

It is the office of the Overlord's Trustman to proclaim his death, as it is his duty to keep death from him.

Lord Buckler was weeping. The tears make glinting tracks down his face but his voice did not waver. He bowed very low to Graycat then walked to the door and opened it wide.

'Overlord Strongmind is dead. Let the Joined Lands mourn him!' he announced to the agitated crowd outside.

Dragonfriend turned to look for Cricket and she too was crying, and so were both healers.

Graycat stood motionless by the bed, her head bowed. Presently she turned away. She did not weep.

She said in a low, fierce voice, as if to herself: 'His courage shall not be wasted. I will find those who set all this in motion and I shall see that they and their plans are destroyed.'

She shook herself a little and raised her voice: 'Dragonfriend – send for Streetskimmer Strongtower and go at once yourself to fetch me Blademistress Medley.'

Amazingly, Dragonfriend hesitated. 'If it please the Young Overlord,' she began, very formally, 'the Remembrancer to the Young Overlord has duties...' she broke off as Graycat turned a blank stare upon her and finished hastily, 'which my apprentice can very well carry out!'

She grabbed Cricket and hissed into his ear, 'Stay with her every moment, understand? Every single moment! And remember everything she says. I'll be as quick as I can. Don't let the Court Remembrancer oust you. He'll do it if he can; he loathes me.'

She thrust him towards Graycat and vanished into the crowd at the door.

So it came about that Cricket Storyteller, an apprentice of a month's standing, attended as the Young Overlord's Remembrancer at the council which summoned the Great Gathering to proclaim the new Overlord.

He felt a complete fraud.

As soon as the councillors were all present, Graycat sent for Russet and Safebide and Yarrow Healer as well as the Healers Agrimony, Goldthread and Ayegreen. Then she spoke to everyone in the room.

'All of you have already, at Lady Jewel's instance, agreed not to speak of the attack upon the Overlord,' she said slowly, looking into their eyes, one by one. 'Now I require your oaths that you will not speak of it to anyone, not even to each other, without my direct command.'

When all the councillors, the healers and the guards had sworn, Graycat suddenly snapped: 'Now. On your oaths, tell me; whom have you told already?'

CHAPTER ELEVEN

There was a shocked hush.

The Young Overlord's gaze passed round the room, then settled upon one of the councillors, a rather prim and self-righteous lord named for his Holding, Fairview. His Use-name was Bothsides, from his habit of saying anxiously: 'One should look at both sides of the question...'

Lord Bothsides would not meet Graycat's eye. He stared at the table, folded and unfolded his hands then jerked himself upright and, looking everywhere but at the Young Overlord, blurted out: 'I did mention the matter to my lady. She had heard such alarming rumours! I had to reassure her...'

Graycat said nothing. She turned her stare on Lady Jewel who thumped both fists on the table.

'Then it's all over the City by now!' she said furiously. 'Lady Twotongues is the most notorious gossip in the whole land.'

Bothsides began to protest but Graycat cut him off. 'Let us discover how much damage has been done,' she said coldly. 'Safebide, will you see if Strongtower has arrived yet?'

Safebide opened the door and at once announced, 'Streetskimmer Strongtower awaits your pleasure, Young Overlord,' and Cricket had his first sight of Dragonfriend's streetskimmer friend.

He slipped into the room, glancing rapidly around, and bowed very low to Graycat. He was, Cricket knew, about his own age, but he was smaller and very thin and wiry. His air of complete self-confidence made it seem only natural that Graycat should treat him as an adult and the equal of her councillors.

'Streetskimmer Strongtower,' she said, 'thank you for coming so swiftly. We need your advice. Tell us what the City says of the Overlord's death.'

Strongtower bowed to the company, though not so low as to Graycat, and replied formally, 'Young Overlord, councillors, it is too soon for the news to have given birth to rumours; everyone is stunned. But there have been tales of the Overlord's illness, many tales and very wild.' He paused and when Graycat nodded to him, went on to detail them.

As he had said, they were wild and so very wide of the mark that Cricket had begun to relax, as much as he could while memorising all Strongtower said, when he added casually, 'And the wildest of all is the tale that the Overlord had a spell cast upon him by the Corulli ambassador. Which is obviously nonsense since the Ambassador is going about his business freely. Only a dafthead would give credit to such a very tall tale.'

He shot a swift glance at Graycat and she looked expressionlessly back.

Cricket remembered the warning Strongtower had sent to Graycat about the Corulli ambassador and wondered how much he guessed. However much that might be, Graycat was clearly not going to confirm his suspicions; but neither did she deny them. She merely thanked him and saying, 'I rely, as always, upon your discretion,' she dismissed him.

He gave her a most un-courtly grin as he bowed and Cricket was sure that he knew far more than he had told them. Cricket watched him swagger to the door. As he left, Strongtower turned and gave him an intense, unsmiling inspection. Cricket sat up straighter, bristling, recalled Dragonfriend's warning and gave him a tiny bow, as between equals. He nodded and slipped away.

'It seems that we have come off very lightly,' said Lady Jewel, still glaring at Bothsides like an infuriated humming bird. She barely came up to his elbow but he was clearly terrified of her. He gulped and mumbled some sort of apology.

'We must remember,' said Graycat coldly, 'that before this

meeting, Lord Fairview had not given his word not to talk. I am quite certain that he will not so much as hint at his knowledge now.'

Looking at Bothsides' face, gleaming with sweat at the steel in the Young Overlord's voice, Cricket felt certain, too. He also felt entirely sure that if anyone else had thought, even fleetingly, of dropping knowing hints, they had discarded the idea at once.

Graycat had sent away all those not of the council and was consulting with the councillors about the proclamation and the days of mourning after the Overlord's funeral, when Dragonfriend's return was reported.

Graycat at once excused herself to the council, beckoned Cricket to follow her, and made for her private rooms so swiftly that he had almost to run to keep up.

Medley and Dragonfriend were waiting for her in the anteroom. Medley, in one of her drab wraparounds, looked puzzled and irritated. Dragonfriend, bright as a dragonfly beside her, clearly was bursting with excitement.

Graycat took Medley into an inner room, leaving the others behind.

Dragonfriend hugged herself, her eyes shining, and whispered, 'I'm sure I'm right! I'm sure Graycat is going to ask Medley to be her Trustman.'

Cricket stared.

'Well, why else would she send me to fetch her?' demanded Dragonfriend. 'Why not one of the Great House messengers or a page, if she wished merely to be polite? One does not, Apprentice Cricket, send the Young Overlord's Remembrancer on casual errands at a time when there are important matters of State to be Remembered! I know I don't look it or act it, as a rule, but I do hold an important office and I do take it seriously.'

She paused and Cricket said hastily, 'I have everything that was said at the council safe in my head, Remembrancer.'

Dragonfriend beamed at him. 'Of course you have, Cricket. Tell me.'

So he told her. He had not been asked for his word to say nothing because Graycat knew he would have to tell Dragonfriend what, as Remembrancer, she ought to know.

She listened with concentration, nodding as he explained his suspicions of Strongtower's knowledge; and finally said, 'Well done, Cricket.'

He relaxed, thankful.

'Now I'll tell you what I've been doing. I stopped on the way to Gather's shop to whistle up one of the streetskimmers who helps her when Medley is out, so that Medley should have no excuse not to leave Gather. I have Strongtower's own code. Any streetskimmer will obey that as they would obey Strongtower himself. Then I got Gather on one side and told her what I thought Medley was wanted for. I knew Medley would not want to come. She doesn't care for the sort of silly hero worship she gets at Court.'

Cricket interrupted her. He couldn't help it. 'Hero worship? You mean – do you really mean she's the Blademistress Medley who captured the Overlord of Westfold all by herself in the war?' he demanded, flabbergasted. That quiet, drab woman? He could hardly believe it.

Dragonfriend looked startled. 'Didn't you know? And there was I thinking how tactful and sensitive you were, not to mention it to her!'

She spluttered with laughter then stopped herself and added, 'But she wasn't quite alone. She had Leg Warrior with her. In his time he's been an under-captain in the army, a sailor, a bandit and now he is Graycat's drillmaster. I'd pick him first for any hopeless venture; and he'd go, grumbling like a thunderstorm but making sure everyone else was safe before he was.'

'He's one of the bandits you told me about, who attacked you and Graycat and Farwalker on your way to the City? The one you said is your friend now?'

'Yes. He thinks the world of Medley. I believe he has asked

her to marry him but I doubt if she'll ever marry; and certainly not if she becomes Trustman.'

'They're taking a long time,' Cricket said, glancing at the closed door. He tried to think of something else to talk about.

'I'm not at all clear what exactly a Trustman does.'

'That depends on what the Overlord wants. The Trustman is not a bodyguard, although it is his right and duty to defend his lord with his own body if needs be. One of Graycat's ancestors was Trustman to an Overlord and got his death taking a sword thrust meant for the Overlord. Then he is the Overlord's friend and, as a rule, not a member of his family. Lord Buckler was born a lord, which means that he is distantly related to the Overlord, as nearly all the lords are, but not closely enough to count as family.

'A Trustman can be a statesman or a warrior or simply the one person the Overlord can relax and be himself with. He can be a lord or a beggar or anything in between. It's not so much what he does, as the sort of person he is.'

'But the Young Overlord – the Overlord has Bull for a bodyguard,' Cricket said uncertainly, thinking of the vast man who dogged Graycat's steps almost everywhere she went.

'Not officially,' Dragonfriend said. 'Bull is self-appointed, and nothing and no one, not even Medley as Trustman will change that.'

'It must be difficult to be a Trustman,' Cricket said slowly, 'and more difficult if you never have been at Court and don't know all the – the tricks of it.'

Dragonfriend nodded. 'That's why they are taking so long. Gray is persuading Medley.'

A sudden thought struck Cricket. 'There can't be many women who would want someone so beautiful casting them in the shade,' he said.

Dragonfriend stared at him, astonished. 'Cast Graycat in the shade? Of course, you don't yet know her very well but, speaking honestly, Cricket, can you really imagine Graycat overshadowed by anyone?'

He had to admit that he could not.

Graycat and Medley came back soon after this. Graycat was smiling slightly but Medley was scowling, as if she had given in against her better judgement. The Young Overlord looked at Dragonfriend and chuckled.

'Yes, Brat, Medley has agreed to become my Trustman. How did you know I meant to ask her?'

'I just knew,' said Dragonfriend vaguely. 'May I congratulate you both?'

Medley shook her head violently. 'I must be insane,' she said, 'or else you are, Gray. And who's to look after Gather?'

'You see?' Dragonfriend turned triumphantly to Cricket. 'Who else calls her Gray? Only me and Farwalker. Now you see why it had to be Medley. As for Gather,' turning back to Medley, 'you can help her pick out one of the youngsters who already work for her, just as she chose you all those years ago. She's pleased about this; and very proud of you.'

'You mean you told her this would happen? Who told you? And how could you know I'd say yes?'

Graycat put an arm around Medley's shoulders.

'No one told her, Medley. She knows us both and she guessed. May I announce your acceptance to the Court now?'

Medley gently pulled herself away from the embrace and sank into the deepest bow possible.

'You have placed your life and your honour into my hands; I place mine in yours. Do whatever seems good to you, my Overlord,' she said.

This was the first time that Graycat had been called by her new title. She looked gravely at Medley's bent head and drew a deep breath, straightening her shoulders as if under a burden.

Then she said cheerfully, 'Very well, then. Come back to the council chamber with me, all of you, and we'll tell them.'

CHAPTER TWELVE

The next few days were full for all of them. Dragonfriend was in constant demand for Remembering and relaying the arrangements for the old Overlord's funeral, while the Court Remembrancer memorised those for the proclamation of the new Overlord which would follow.

Cricket thought it hard that Dragonfriend should have the sad task and the Court Remembrancer, an embittered old man called Longwit, should have the happy one.

'After all,' he urged, 'you are the Young Overlord's Remembrancer; you should be the one to organise her proclamation.'

Dragonfriend shook her head. 'No, Cricket. Longwit is jealous enough of me as it is. He is a failed storyteller and no storyteller, no matter how important the office, would prefer to be a master Remembrancer rather than a master Storyteller. I am both.'

She gave him one of her level stares. 'Would not you be jealous, Cricket Storyteller, if one of your friends in Edgescarp suddenly turned up here as the apprentice of, say, the Storyteller? And then became a master Storyteller while you were not even a journeyman?'

He thought about it. 'Yes, I suppose I should. But I'd still be a storyteller and your apprentice. And when you are the Storyteller –' he broke off at the appalled expression on her face.

'Never, never say that again!' She swallowed painfully and, seeing his bewilderment, said in a dry whisper: 'Cricket, I can *never* be the Storyteller. I lost my Storyteller Name. I shall never even be considered for it. No matter if I were as great a Storyteller as Goldentongue himself; the stain is too – is too –' she stopped, not attempting to hide the tears sliding down her face.

Cricket would rather have bitten out his tongue than hurt her so and now he could not even say he was sorry for fear of making it worse. He pulled a kerchief from his pouch – clean, for a wonder, and pushed it into her hand. As her fingers closed on it, he bent very hastily and kissed them. Then he ran.

All Cricket wanted at that moment was somewhere to hide. He found his feet leading him down to the cells, where Dreamtalker was imprisoned. He was about to turn back when he was struck by the deep silence in the long passage. There should have been some noise, the sounds of men moving around, perhaps voices. But there was nothing.

He held his breath to listen harder. Still nothing. He crept forward cautiously to peer round the turn of the passage, where the first group of guards had been stationed. There was nobody there. Puzzled, and beginning to be alarmed, he tiptoed on. There should be another set of guards within eyeshot of the cell.

He turned the corner and the passage was empty. So was the cell. The lanterns shone steadily on its space. There was the bed, the table, even the candles, burnt down to stubs and guttering out; but no Dreamtalker and no guards.

Cricket stood and stared. Surely he should have heard if the hypnotist had been released? Or would Graycat have thought it none of his business? But Dragonfriend would have been told, for certain. He caught his breath in terror and began to run, flat out, back to their rooms.

When he skidded into Dragonfriend's suite it was empty. Of course, she had to attend the council meeting with Graycat. He stood gulping air, wondering what to do, who to tell. He must tell somebody but it must be someone who already knew about Dreamtalker. Whether he had escaped or been released, Graycat would not want the news spread abroad.

Lord Farwalker? He was not in the Great House today. Lady Jewel? She would be in council, too, and Cricket would not be allowed in. One of the healers! Agrimony had gone back to his own practice in the City, but if he could find Ayegreen or Goldthread or even Yarrow... and no one is surprised at a healer being sought in a hurry. And Ayegreen, especially, could and would break in on the council if she thought it necessary. Goldthread was more likely to hesitate and quote rules and be punctilious.

Cricket ran out into the corridor again and stopped a page. He did not know where Ayegreen was but, seeing Cricket's anxiety, sent him to another who might know. He fled along corridor after corridor, trying to keep calm, cursing the builders who had made the place so large and so intricate, until at last he found Healer Ayegreen.

Cricket had almost no breath left but he dragged her far enough away from any listeners and gasped out what he had discovered. To his horror Ayegreen did not reply. She stood for several moments staring blankly at him as if she had no idea what he was talking about.

Then she said, 'You say you must speak to the Overlord at once? You want me to get you into the council chamber?'

Cricket opened his mouth to say that he hadn't said anything of the sort, though he did, in fact, want her help to reach Graycat; when he suddenly remembered the terms of the oath she and the others had sworn: not to speak of the hypnotising even among themselves without Graycat's direct order. Cricket had not sworn. He could tell Ayegreen about it, but she could not reply, at least not directly.

He said: 'I do need your help to reach the Overlord quickly.'

'What are we waiting for?' said Ayegreen and set off briskly for the council chamber.

The Door wards let them through at once. Ayegreen merely said to them: 'Emergency. The Overlord must be informed at once.' and the doors were flung open and she was announced. They did not bother with Cricket, for which he was grateful.

All the councillors turned at the interruption and Cricket felt like hiding in Ayegreen's narrow shadow; he was still not used to being stared at.

Then Graycat said, 'Ayegreen! Is something wrong? You have leave to speak,' she added as Ayegreen did not immediately answer.

'Am I ordered to speak, my Overlord?' Ayegreen said, with slow significance, and Cricket saw Dragonfriend move sharply.

Graycat looked puzzled and Dragonfriend whispered to her urgently. Graycat cast a hasty glance around the councillors.

There were some present who had not been at the council when Dreamtalker's attack had been discussed. They knew nothing about him and Cricket could see that Graycat had no mind to tell them.

She rose and said, 'Medley, will you take my place for a while? I shall return soon.' and while the councillors were still gasping, she beckoned to Dragonfriend and led Ayegreen and Cricket from the Chamber.

The Door wards were waved aside and Graycat said in a low voice, 'My order is that you speak what you know.'

'It's what Cricket here knows,' said Ayegreen, grimly. 'I was merely his messenger.'

Graycat looked at him and waited. His teeth were chattering by now but he stiffened his jaw muscles and said, without any respectful salutations, 'Has Dreamtalker been released?'

Dragonfriend shuddered. Graycat said slowly, her eyes fast on his, 'I have given no orders for his release.'

'Then he's escaped. All the guards are gone and his cell is empty,' Cricket told her, the words sounding strange and meaningless in his mouth.

The under-captain in charge of the guards detailed to watch Dreamtalker was totally bewildered when Graycat had him brought to her private rooms.

'But when the prisoner was so sick, the healer said he must be moved; and the healer had your ring and the password, my Overlord!' he protested.

'Which healer?' Graycat asked him.

'Why, the little old one, Healer Agrimony. We knew him, so...'

'Tell me what happened. From the beginning, Under-captain Hardhand.'

The under-captain swallowed nervously. 'Well, first off, the prisoner started groaning. He sort of staggered to the bars and held on to them all doubled up, then he spewed all over the passage. So I went to see what was wrong. What else could I do? And then I looked back and there was the healer coming up the passage, you see, so I calls out to the men to bring him over to the cell, you see, and he looks the prisoner over and he says, "Can't treat him here," he says. "Get this door open sharp and carry him out," he says.'

'And so you unlocked the cell door?' put in Graycat.

'Well, I had to, to let the healer get at him, you see. But first I says to him, "My orders are that no one's to go in that cell," and then he shows me the ring and he says, "Here's the Overlord's own signet," which I recognised all right, and then I says "What about the password?" and he gives the password, just like you told us, my lady, and so I let him in.

'Then he tells two of my men to help him lift the prisoner and they carry him out and the healer says to me, "Better get that mess cleaned up, then you can all go off duty." So that's what we done.'

Graycat shut her eyes. 'Stars! What a fool!' she exclaimed. 'No, not you, Hardhand, myself. I should have warned you against such a ploy. Once he had you close he could make you hear and see whatever he chose. Healer Agrimony was not there at all. He has not been in the Great House for days. You only thought you saw the ring – here it is on my finger – and imagined you heard the password. Did he even really vomit, I wonder?'

Cricket recalled sniffing at a sour unpleasantness in the dungeon. 'Yes, for I smelled it,' he told her. 'That much must have been real.'

'Easy enough for him to thrust his fingers down his throat and make himself vomit,' said Ayegreen. 'He has been a healer; he'd know.'

'Well.' Graycat ran her hands through her hair. 'That's that. I don't see how we can ever catch him now. But why, I wonder, did he take such a risk just at this moment? Or... Under-captain! Did he know of the Overlord's death?'

The guards, it seemed, had told him. They had also told him that Graycat blamed him for the death of her great-uncle and would 'get around to him quite soon'. He had evidently believed them, believed that his life was in danger, and had fled to escape a probably lingering death.

Graycat's eyes narrowed. Hardhand shrank from the anger in her face and Cricket didn't blame him.

She said, very carefully, as if afraid to say too much, 'Those men who amused themselves in this way are confined to their quarters until I have leisure to deal with them. Under-captain Hardhand, you did not stop their fun, did you?'

Hardhand hesitated. 'N-not at once, Overlord,' he stammered. 'I-I reckoned he deserved to be scared a bit.'

'Yes. And what should your own punishment be, do you think?' asked Graycat softly. To Cricket's surprise, he stood up straight and stared back at her.

'Greater than theirs, Overlord,' he said, 'It was up to me, wasn't it? I was in charge.'

Graycat nodded.

'You are demoted. Not for allowing the prisoner to escape but for allowing him to be driven to the attempt,' she said. 'You were responsible, as you say, and you did not exercise your responsibility. No officer, whether he is the commander in chief or an under-captain, who does not know when and how to do this, is fit to be an officer. When you think you are fit, ask to speak with me again.'

She sent him away, summoned the captain of her own guard, told him of the demotion and that some men were confined to quarters and dismissed him, all absent-mindedly as if thinking hard about something else.

When Captain Sureshield had gone, she turned to Cricket.

'Now, Cricket. We have no more hope of questioning Dreamtalker. You are now our only possible witness. Tell me again what you were saying when the Overlord cried out and died.'

CHAPTER THIRTEEN

Healer Agrimony and Cricket had both already told Graycat all that they had said in the Overlord's hearing just before he died. But Cricket did not say so. He merely repeated it again, word for word. He still could not see what, in their talk about storytellers and his own future plans, could possibly have made the Overlord wake and cry out. All the same, he had called out his refusal just as Cricket spoke of the Wilders and their gildentrees.

Graycat had worried at this before, like a dog with a too large bone; now she went over it all again.

Presently, 'I have sent messengers to the Wilders,' she told them, 'asking if they have news of anything unusual or out of place or any rumour, no matter how far-fetched. There has not yet been time for a reply. They have pigeons, but you can send very little news by a pigeon.'

She drummed her fingers restlessly on her desk and suddenly stopped. 'Great Stars!' she exclaimed. 'I told Medley I'd be back shortly. Stay here, you two, and try if you can come up with some ideas. Stay or go as you wish, Healer. I don't suppose I'll be long – the meeting must almost have ended!' and she whirled out.

Dragonfriend and Cricket exchanged glances and snorted with suppressed laughter, remembering the shocked faces in the council chamber. Ayegreen shook her head at them and took her leave, saying that she had work to do. Cricket thanked her for her help with real gratitude.

They sat and stared at each other. Cricket's mind was a blank. He could think of nothing – except...

'Dragonfriend, tell me all about the Gilden Forest and the gildentrees!' he said eagerly.

She gave him a puzzled look but, making no comment, settled herself on one of the big floor cushions.

'Long, long ago,' she began, 'when men first came to live in these lands, the gildentrees were not protected. They were cut down in their hundreds and thousands for the strength and beauty of their wood which made the timber from just one tree worth a lord's ransom. The doors of this Great House are made of gildenwood, and are hundreds of years older than the House; indeed the House was built around them! They are worth more than the whole City, Cricket.

'Now the gildentrees grow slowly; and there are male and female trees, just as with holly, so not all the trees bear the berries and the seeds within them. Again, many of the seeds never sprout and many seedlings die before they have rooted properly.

'Thus it was that the men of those times did not at first realise that, although they collected seeds and sowed them in other places and dug up seedlings and replanted them likewise, thinking to have plantations of gildentrees, yet the seeds never grew and the seedlings all died. When they found this out, they tried to transplant larger, healthy saplings but these did not flourish and would die in a year or two.

'The lords of the lands bordering the Gilden Forest had profited greatly by the sale of the timber. They had opposed the attempts to plant the trees elsewhere, because they wished to keep all in their hands, so many of them were pleased at the failures.

'But there were some who were wiser. Suppose some disease should attack the Gilden Forest? All the trees might die and where would the profits be then?

'Now, while the wise lords were making tests and the foolish lords were trying to prevent them, men were stealing into the forest and felling the trees in secret. When the lords knew this, they left off quarrelling and agreed that the forest must be protected or there would be no trees left to sell. Already there were great areas bare of trees and going to scrub.

'So the youngest son of one of the lords was sent with men, a few from among the followers of each lord, to patrol the forest and guard the trees. These men, led by the lord's son, who was later called Treelover, gradually came to be the trees' champions and to care for them far beyond their original orders.

'They cleared away the scrub and they collected seeds and seedlings to replace the old trees that had been felled and they carried water for their young tender trees in time of drought.

'They also discovered that the gildenberries could be eaten and were so delicious that high prices would be paid for them, so that not so many trees need be cut. And the guardians were so fierce and terrible in their defence of the forest that very soon not the most fearless outlaw would attempt to fell a gildentree.

'Then Treelover, through the deaths of his brothers, unexpectedly inherited his father's lordship and lands. With his Overlord's permission, he gave all the lands to be divided between the other lords who had a claim upon the gildentrees. In exchange for these lands, he was given the right to say which trees and how many should be felled, throughout the forest. He renounced any profits from the timber.

'This seemed madness to the other lords, but Treelover knew what he was about. He asked, in addition, that all new trees should belong to him. Since the trees are so slow to grow, only bearing fruit after thirty years and are not fit to cut for another twenty, this meant that he could not fell any of his own trees for at least fifty years; and the other lords laughed and agreed.

'But Treelover and his men had long sought for the reason of the trees' dying. They had even transplanted full grown trees, only to find that as soon as their roots reached beyond the soil that had been moved with them, they too began to die. They had come to believe that it was something in the soil of the Gilden Forest which the trees needed and which existed nowhere else.

'And indeed to this day no one has ever found out what it

is and all efforts to find soil elsewhere in which the trees can flourish, have failed.

'Therefore all the trees in the forest would eventually belong to Treelover – or rather to his heirs – and, as none would grow anywhere else, that meant all the gildentrees in the world!

'So Treelover and his family and his foresters and their families and all their descendants became the Wilders and although some of them live in other forests and are the finest foresters in the world, most of them live in the Gilden Forest and tend the gildentrees, which are never felled save to thin out the forest or unless they have been damaged or diseased or are very near the end of their long life.'

She finished and waited, looking at Cricket enquiringly. He hesitated. It was such a weird idea that had jolted him; but perhaps...

He took a deep breath and said in a rush: 'Suppose someone wanted to steal gildenwood and suppose that, in order to have some sort of law on their side, they hired Dreamtalker to make the Overlord give them a kind of permission? Yes, I know he couldn't give them a legal right to the timber,' and, as Dragonfriend began to protest, 'But think – what would happen if a gang of woodmen simply started felling gildentrees, on the Joined Lands side of the forest, and told anyone who found them that they had the Overlord's permission? Maybe showed his ring or something of the sort? Wouldn't the Wilders or the Borderers or whoever caught them send to the Overlord to check? And suppose the answer came back that Yes, the Overlord had given them leave?'

'But what would they have gained?' protested Dragonfriend. 'Sooner or later someone would say it was nonsense and the Overlord had no rights in the matter. Then they would be in trouble up to the chin.'

'Time – they'd gain time to fell and steal more trees!' Cricket told her. 'You told me once that the Wilders carry no weapons and take no sides in war. Could they stop a whole gang of armed men?'

'The wolves...' began Dragonfriend; and paused. 'You may be right,' she said slowly. 'Bowmen could hold off the wolves, I suppose. At least for a time.' She shook her head. 'I don't know. It doesn't feel quite right, somehow. And yet it fits most of the facts we have.'

'What doesn't it fit?' Cricket asked but she refused to answer, saying that Graycat must be told first.

'You must not speak of this to anyone else,' she said seriously.

Cricket suddenly felt stifled with secrets. 'I wish we were still on the road,' he said miserably. 'I don't like it here with all these mysteries and secrets. You and Lord Farwalker and Overlord Graycat have secrets between you that I mustn't know; and the councillors have more that I know and mustn't tell; and now there's this that I can't tell anyone but you and the Overlord. And I never know why!'

'Oh, Cricket, I'm sorry!' Storyteller Wolftalker Dragonfriend looked at him ruefully, trying not to laugh. He scowled at her and she said penitently, 'No, really, I am! In all truth it is serious; but if you could have seen your face! Now, listen, Cricket and I shall tell you as much as I may.'

She switched to speaking in the Elder tongue and, even so, lowered her voice.

'There are certain folk, landholders mostly but some of the greater traders also, who did not like Overlord Strongmind's choice of Graycat as his heir. The Great Gathering agreed that she should be the Young Overlord, it is true; but now it is being said that the Overlord tricked the Gathering into accepting her. And that he used the excitement of the Fulfilled Prophecy and the attempt on her life by Lord Freeforest to call for agreement while everyone was full of emotion and not thinking straight. So they say. And,' she held up a hand to silence his shocked protest, 'they are absolutely correct. That is exactly what the Overlord did.'

She smiled at his startled horror.

'Did you think, my apprentice, that because Graycat is wise and strong and most fitted to be Overlord, everyone hailed her with joy and relief? Oh, no. They hailed her – I was there and watched it happen – because her great-uncle was a very clever old man who used circumstances to push the Gathering in the direction he chose.

'For the good of the Joined Lands, he had decided that his great-niece, the outlaw Graycat, should become his successor; and the luck which has always attended Graycat held, right up to Freeforest's craziness. That assassination attempt was the luckiest thing that could have happened, though I promise you I did not think so when I saw that dreadful knife being thrust at her back! Not one person in the High Chamber stopped to think after that. They just cheered for Graycat. The Overlord even got away with rewarding Farwalker, when he had just broken all law and custom by shooting down Freeforest in the Overlord's presence.

'No, Cricket, Graycat's enemies are right. They were bamboozled and tricked. However, they did agree, they did acclaim her, not one of them spoke up in protest later at her proclamation and,' she finished viciously, 'not one of them now has a leg to stand upon.'

CHAPTER FOURTEEN

Cricket was silent, trying to absorb this.

'But why is it a secret?' he asked at last, wondering if he'd perhaps missed some of her meaning in the still, to him, strange Elder tongue. 'Surely everyone who was there knows what happened? I don't understand.'

'Graycat's enemies understand how they were led by the nose. Most of the others do not. And it will be well for our new Overlord that they never do; or not until after her proclamation, at least,' said the Overlord's Storyteller, grimly. 'There is still time for rivals, Cricket. Still time for oh, someone like Lady Deepskill's son, Wolfbane, to set himself up as a candidate. It could divide the Joined Lands. Merely the story of the old Overlord's death, if it were all told, might sow the seeds of revolt.'

She sighed and reverted to the Common speech. 'You know, Cricket, in spite of what Farwalker said about the unrest in the Seaward Hills, I still think it was intended to get Graycat out of the City.'

The door behind them closed. 'So do I,' said Graycat, coming softly to them. 'And now I have more news for you, storytellers. A message pigeon arrived just now. The High Overlord is sending his herald, not only to attend my proclamation, but to bring some message which he will deliver to the Great Gathering. What under Sky that young man thinks he is doing I do not know! I'm afraid we shan't have time to welcome the herald correctly. He will arrive on the very day of the funeral.'

'Did you decide on the day for the funeral before, or after, you got the High Overlord's message?' asked Dragonfriend slyly.

Graycat looked innocent. 'I wonder what made you ask that,'

she said, and smiled. 'Now, what ideas have you two storytellers thought of?'

They told her.

She became serious at once. 'Yes, I see what you mean, Cricket,' she said thoughtfully, 'but I understand Dragonfriend's feeling as well. There is something else, I'm sure of it. This has a feel about it of something more subtle than mere theft, even the theft of gildentrees.'

'What can we do about the gildentrees, then?' Cricket asked.

Graycat frowned. 'Wait. Wait for the Wilders to reply, wait to see what this herald wants and then...'

'Then Cricket and I go to the Gilden Forest and see for ourselves!' said Dragonfriend eagerly. 'Well, I meant to take or send him soon. Plenty of people know that. It shouldn't arouse any suspicion. It's ideal!'

She was speaking in such a rush that Graycat actually had to clap a hand over her mouth to silence her.

'Storyteller Wolftalker Dragonfriend,' said The Overlord sternly, 'I once said that you need never ask me for permission to come or go; and I have not the least intention of taking back my promise. But, my Remembrancer, my Storyteller, let me warn you, you shall not, while I can prevent it, run your head blindly into a noose. Have you even thought of the danger you might lead your apprentice into if his suspicions are correct? You have no caution, have you? You still expect all to go well for you. I suppose it is because you storytellers have a sheltered upbringing.'

Dragonfriend stared at her in amazed indignation.

'Sheltered?' she gasped.

Graycat smiled and looked at Cricket. 'Tell her, Cricket Farmer's son,' she said.

Of course, she knew about living as a peasant. She had done so more than once while she was outlawed.

Cricket swallowed. 'You said, Dragonfriend, when you were telling me about how you met Lord Farwalker, that you were near starving,' he said hesitantly. 'Well, I didn't say so then, because – well, because it didn't seem – I mean, I didn't want to spoil the story – but I do know what it feels like to be nearly starving. We go hungry most winters; not for days, but for weeks, and of course, it isn't so bad when everyone is hungry and in our village we share alike. You were alone, and that must feel worse. And our lord is not like Lord Eaglon but sometimes, when we go to market, there are rich people and we – they despise us and so we – we don't go in the taverns or the eating houses. That's why I did so want to eat at the inn in Scarp-end. I'd never dared to before but I knew they wouldn't be nasty to a storyteller...'

He ran out of breath and found he was twisting his hands together. Dragonfriend caught them in both of hers. 'Oh, Cricket, I'm sorry! I'd have stopped to eat in Scarp-end if I'd known.'

He saw that she cared as much for his disappointment as he had.

She turned back to Graycat. 'Yes, I see what you mean. We do avoid a lot of misery, don't we? Safely tucked up in our cosy storytellers' immunity.'

Graycat smiled at her. 'Well, my friend, do you still intend to take your apprentice to the Gilden Forest?'

Dragonfriend hesitated. 'What do you think, Cricket? You'd be in danger too, if we are right.'

'I think we ought to go,' he told her, feeling wonderfully pleased at being consulted. 'But couldn't someone go with us? Speedhand, say?'

'Well thought on, Cricket, but we must keep this between those who already know the truth, as far as possible,' said Graycat. 'Dragonfriend, suppose Speedhand does go with you. How much can you safely tell him?'

'That there are rumours of outlaws in the Gilden Forest. So much is true and so much he will need to know,' said Dragonfriend. 'I trust him entirely but I'll not burden him further.'

Graycat nodded. 'Publicly, I can send him on detached duty or, better, order him to take leave on the grounds that his arm is still weak.'

'He'll not care to have his friends thinking he is a weakling,' said Dragonfriend, grinning. Graycat looked at them and became the Overlord again.

'He will do as he is told,' she said, flatly.

'But not till after the proclamation,' said Dragonfriend. 'Nobody would believe it if I went before.'

'The funeral is to be the day after tomorrow,' said Graycat. 'The proclamation will be a week after that. You could leave later that week; let's say two days after the proclamation. If, that is, we have not heard from the Wilders that it is all true. Then I shall be sending an army, not two children and one Swordsman.'

'And when will the herald of the High Overlord address the great gathering?' asked Dragonfriend, in a subdued voice.

'Three days after the funeral.' Graycat sighed and suddenly looked so tired that Cricket nudged Dragonfriend and started to edge towards the door. They made their bows and left her, seated at her desk and frowning as she leafed through a pile of notes about the funeral arrangements.

'I'm glad storytellers don't read or write,' Cricket told Dragonfriend. 'Aren't you? But why did Graycat call the High Overlord "that young man"?'

Dragonfriend grinned. 'He is exactly the same age as she is,' she said, 'but when he became High Overlord ten years ago, he was only twenty. Everyone still thinks of him as very young.'

'They'll have to start thinking differently soon. Thirty is pretty old,' Cricket remarked.

The funeral of Overlord Strongmind was attended by his closest friends, his nearest kin and his council, most of whom were either friends or kindred. And by almost the entire City and as many of the country folk from twenty miles around as could cram themselves into the City.

Cricket went to stand in the Great Avenue with Carter Stark, Gather and a small group of streetskimmers, all of whom were vying for Stark's attention.

But even they fell silent when the funeral procession came slowly through the crowded streets. Graycat, bareheaded and all in black, led the single horse that drew a small tilt cart.

On the cart lay the old Overlord, in a perfectly plain wooden coffin.

The cart was wreathed with wild flowers but the coffin was bare, save for the ebony and crystal Staff of the Domain lying on top of it. The staff rolled a little with the movement of the cart and Lord Buckler, Strongmind's Trustman, walking beside the cart, was keeping an eye on it in case it rolled too far.

Medley walked on the other side but all her attention was on Graycat; Cricket saw that this was how it would be for her now, until one or other of them died. He did not know which to feel sorrier for, Lord Buckler or Blademistress Medley.

The funeral procession passed them. Cricket saw Dragonfriend walking between Silkentongue and his wife Sweetvoice, not far behind the coffin.

Lord Farwalker was quite a long way back and Cricket wondered if this was because he was no kin at all to the old Overlord or if there was some other reason. Lady Jewel and the other members of the council had been directly behind the coffin.

He wondered also how they had kept Bull away. Graycat's bodyguard was almost her shadow and it was rumoured that he always slept across her doorway, so devoted was he to her. Then he realised that the disturbance he had noticed on the other side of the street, keeping pace with the head of the procession, must have been Bull. For such a big man he moved very lightly.

The tail of the procession passed and many in the crowd closed in behind it and followed through the streets to the south-western end of the City, where New Bridge gave on to the Outwall Valley and the burial ground.

Gather patted Cricket's hand and asked if he wanted to follow, too; but he told her that he'd rather go home with her, if she would like it. She was so frail that he was worried about her.

Stark and her swirl of streetskimmers were drawn after the crowd. Gather and Cricket turned back towards her shop. So it happened that he was the one who saw the herald of the High Overlord arrive in the City by the Great East Bridge just as the funeral left it by the western one.

CHAPTER FIFTEEN

'They didn't look annoyed,' Cricket told Dragonfriend when she returned to the Great House. 'I only saw them from a distance, of course, and maybe the guards on the Great Bridge didn't tell them that everyone had gone to the funeral. I didn't follow them to the Great House; I took Gather home.'

'Quite right. Well, I can't tell you anything more. Gray just sent them a message of greeting when we got back.' Dragonfriend yawned and stretched, then came suddenly alert again.

'Oh, Stars! I'd forgotten; I'll have to be at the welcoming banquet tonight and I feel worn out.'

Cricket yawned in sympathy and they both laughed.

'Have a rest now and I'll wake you in time to dress,' Cricket suggested.

He had made friends with some of the pages by now and while Dragonfriend rested he went to gather any gossip he could. He already knew that the herald and his immediate followers had been given the suite of rooms which belonged to the Overlord. The pages told him that some of the councillors felt that Graycat was doing them too great an honour.

A whole company of guards had been called up from the Keep to watch over the herald and his people.

'They spend most of their time chasing curious folk away from the strangers!' said Cricket's friends, giggling. Buckthorn, his best friend among the pages, was betting that none of the nosy visitors would manage to speak to the herald or indeed any of his following, until after the Great Gathering. 'If then!' said Buckthorn. Most of the pages refused the wager. Then, 'A storyteller would have a better chance!' one of them suggested;

and somehow Cricket found that he had bet a larger sum than he owned that he would speak with one of the High Overlord's men within the next twenty-four hours.

Cricket went back to wake Dragonfriend, wondering how he could possibly do it, or have been such an idiot as to agree to try.

He had no chance to make the attempt that evening. All the High Overlord's people were at the banquet, and they had been turned out of Dragonfriend's rooms which were needed for the crowd of visiting lords, not all of whom owned TownHolds in the City. Graycat had allotted rooms in her suite to Medley, Bull, Dragonfriend and Cricket.

Then, in the morning, Graycat sat quietly in the Young Overlord's private apartments and Dragonfriend kept Cricket busy memorising the names of the lords and landholders who were arriving for the Overlord's proclamation. Cricket hadn't a moment to himself. By noon he was nearly desperate: and still the lords and ladies came to pay their respects and the storytellers Remembered them.

Medley, too, would have preferred far fewer landholders. She disliked the crowd in the Great House. Graycat was very silent and unsmiling, patient, but in a manner which left Cricket wondering if she was really aware of anyone. Medley was seldom far from Graycat's side. Bull, as usual, scarcely left her. Cricket thought they were worried about her but when he mentioned it to Dragonfriend; she told him that now Graycat had the time, she was silently mourning the Overlord.

'He was her nearest relative,' she explained. 'Of course, Lady Deepskill is a cousin but only of the half blood and I don't think there are any kin of her father, Lord Ironmind, closer than third cousin.'

'I don't even know what a third cousin is,' Cricket confessed. 'You storytellers are crazed on relationships.'

Dragonfriend looked startled. 'You mean you don't know who your cousins are?'

'Most of Edgescarp, I suppose, but who cares?' Cricket said. 'Why worry?'

Dragonfriend shook her head. 'You are a storyteller now, Cricket. You'll have to start learning the degrees of relationship, if only because the Lords need them for inheritance. Do you know, I can recite my own mother's line right back to the Lady Dragonfriend, the Last Sorceress! That's twenty-three generations; and my father's for nineteen.'

He stared, dumbstruck.

'Don't you believe me?' Dragonfriend laughed and began to recite: 'My mother was Beechenhair, daughter of Amber, daughter of Anytale, daughter of Featherfern, daughter of Fleetwind, daughter of Starrise, daughter of Stormcloud...'

'I believe you, I believe you!' Cricket said hurriedly. 'Storytellers don't lie. I know that. I was just, um, overawed by the great antiquity of...'

Dragonfriend dug him hard in the ribs and he doubled up, giggling.

That afternoon was his last chance to win his bet. He got no further than the outer door of the suite, and had his ears boxed for his pains. The guards were getting irritable.

Dragonfriend had no sympathy for him. 'You're an idiot, Cricket,' she told him. 'We shall both of us be at the Gathering. You'll have plenty of chances to stare at them then.'

She did not know about the bet, and he had no intention of telling her. The trouble was that he had lost his bet and had nothing like enough to pay with. Buckthorn didn't know that he had won yet, but Cricket would have to tell him soon. He did some hard thinking and went to see Streetskimmer Strongtower.

Strongtower was highly amused. Cricket set his teeth and refused to lose his temper. He was here as a beggar and could not afford to get angry. And he remembered Dragonfriend's warning. Only a fool would challenge Strongtower on his own ground.

'You'd never make a streetskimmer,' he said, laughing. 'You have something to sell, you dafthead! You're a storyteller, aren't you? Tell stories, then! You'll soon earn enough to pay your tiny debt.'

Cricket stood gaping, feeling quite as foolish as he'd said.

Then he remembered something. 'But I'm only an apprentice,' he protested. 'I'd need to ask Dragonfriend's permission. And then she'll want to know why...'

Strongtower grinned. 'I'll ask her leave,' he promised. 'I'll say the streetskimmers want a story and it will be good practice for you. It will, too! Streetskimmers are a hard audience to please. But we'll pay you anyhow.'

Cricket gulped. He wondered what would happen if he failed to please. Would the money be thrown in the gutter for him to pick out of the filth? Or would he get beaten up? What sort of tale or story would they ask for?

By the time Strongtower came for him, late next afternoon, Cricket was in a sweat of worry and had gone over every story he could remember. In a daze, he followed Strongtower to the disused warehouse by the river that was the streetskimmers' meeting place. There must have been fifty or more ragged streetskimmers waiting for him.

He asked them what story they wanted.

They wanted his own.

So, thoroughly shaken and quite unprepared, Cricket told it to them. He began with his longing to be a storyteller and finished with the scene in the storytellers' Guildhall when Gaingold was renamed Gainscorn. He told how the man was expelled from the storytellers and, although Cricket still felt sick at the thought of his horrible fate, he gave the sentencing in full.

They listened in total silence, all attention. They were a wonderful audience and Cricket found himself wondering why Strongtower had claimed that they were hard to please; until they started cross-questioning him about all sorts of minor points.

'Why don't you say which tales Spring Rain told you?' and 'Why put in the name Dragonfriend gave your pony? It's not needful for us to know that.'

'But I didn't expect to be asked for my own Story!' he protested.

Finally, 'It was well enough for a first try,' pronounced the skinny child who had brought Strongtower's warning to Dragonfriend. She smiled at him, kindly. 'You'll do better next time.'

Strongtower grinned at Cricket's expression. He had collected a handful of coins from the streetskimmers and was counting them rapidly.

Suddenly he stopped and frowned. 'Who put in a false copper?' he demanded sharply. There was an alarmed hush. Then a very small boy stood up, trembling visibly.

'I – I hadn't got nothing else,' he whispered.

Strongtower beckoned him forward. 'You can't pay a storyteller with a bad coin,' he said severely and handed it back to him. 'Who gave it to you, Minnow?' he added, casually.

Minnow described the man carefully. The others listened with great concentration.

'A stranger,' one of them said. 'No one known to us would cheat one of Strongtower's folk,' with such calm assurance that Cricket was reminded strongly of Medley's quiet self-confidence.

Strongtower grinned at him, nodded agreement and solemnly begged Minnow to exchange the false coin for a good one of his own.

'I shall see to this affair for you,' he promised. 'Now you may pay the storyteller,' and the boy, beaming with satisfaction, gave Cricket his only coin and the rest of the money Strongtower had collected.

He could hardly bear to take it but Strongtower obviously expected him to; so Cricket accepted his first fee with thanks. It was more than enough to pay his debt.

When he told Dragonfriend about it that evening, confessing

to his bet at the same time, she drew in her breath sharply. 'Cricket – thank the Stars you took it! If you had refused their money, you would have given the streetskimmers an intolerable insult. You'd have been lucky to escape with a thrashing!'

Next morning Cricket paid Buckthorn as soon as he could find him, which was not easy as the Gathering was to be at noon and the pages were very busy. Buckthorn was too excited to remark on how slow Cricket had been; he stuffed the coins in his pouch and dashed away to the Master of Pages, who was calling loudly for more messengers.

Cricket made his way back to the Young Overlord's suite, where he got a tongue-lashing from Dragonfriend for disappearing. He was astonished. Then he understood.

He was still cocooned in the glow of his yesterday's success but she was nervous!

It was catching. When they entered the High Chamber a little before noon he felt shivers run down his spine.

CHAPTER SIXTEEN

The High Chamber was not called High for nothing. It was a huge room, two tall storeys high, with galleries running round it at the first storey level. Stairs led up to these from the floor of the Chamber at intervals, but the galleries could be reached from other parts of the Great House as well.

The daylight entered by shafts slanting down from the roof, for the Chamber was almost buried inside the Great House and had no outside walls where windows might be set. The walls were covered with long narrow hangings of plain linen cloth, some bleached to a silvery white, others left unbleached. The effect was like being in a field of ripe barley when the wind blows across it.

At night, Dragonfriend told Cricket, it looked even more splendid, for it was lit by torches set in holders fixed at head height all round the room.

'But a daylight Gathering saves a lot of trouble,' she remarked, with a determinedly practical air, 'for the torches always leave sooty streaks on the hangings and then they have to be cleaned. It's a tremendous business, especially in winter.'

Cricket was not to sit with Dragonfriend. She had her official seat beside the dais where the Overlord's chair of state was placed, at the northern end of the chamber, facing the main doors down the length of the room. They had slipped in by the Overlord's private door behind the dais and Dragonfriend let Cricket stand for a while and stare round the High Chamber, as it filled with colour and noise.

None of the landholders and guildmasters seemed to be

awed to silence as he was. They were greeting friends or arguing, settling themselves in their seats or wandering round looking for a space; and all looking as bright and sounding as noisy as so many parrots.

'You're to sit up in that gallery,' Dragonfriend told him. 'Near enough to watch the herald's followers, when he is speaking to the Gathering. Silkentongue wants to know everything you can find out from the way they behave. Watch their hands and the way they stand and move, not just the faces. Now, hurry, or you'll miss your place. The Steward will be letting people into the galleries soon.'

'You make it sound as though the herald's folk are dangerous, perhaps have some sort of designs upon Graycat. Do you think..?'

'No, no! Silkentongue simply wants to be sure that what they say is what they mean. He is not afraid of any plot against Gray. At least,' Dragonfriend sounded suddenly doubtful, 'he hasn't said anything to me. Anyway,' she added briskly, 'there will be lots of storytellers all round the Chamber, so you need not fear that everything rests on your shoulders. Just keep your eyes open.

'And, Cricket, before you go; Strongtower tells me he thinks well of your storytelling. He isn't easily impressed, so – my congratulations, Storyteller!'

Cricket almost fell over his own feet on the stairs up to the gallery, he was so overcome. Strongtower must have taken the trouble to come up to the Great House that morning especially to tell Dragonfriend that he had done well! He sat beaming from ear to ear in a haze of goodwill while the landholders and guildmasters filled the hall below.

Then he was jerked to the alert again.

The Overlord's fanfare sounded, everyone stopped talking and stood up, the door behind the dais swung wide and Graycat appeared. She did not pause but moved quietly forward to her chair of state. Behind her and one pace to her left was Medley.

They both wore the Overlord's black and silver; but Graycat, still in mourning for her great-uncle, wore a plain black robe in heavy linen with a narrow silver sash as the only relief, while Medley blazed and glittered.

Her robe was of shining black silk embroidered all over with silver in intricate swirling patterns. A long silver scarf covering her high piled hair was knotted tightly behind her head, with the ends falling forward over her shoulders. Whenever she moved her head the silver flowed and gleamed, eye-catching. Her robes stirred to her least movement and the patterned silver slid in waves across her body. Graycat was eclipsed.

It took Cricket longer than it should have to understand that this was deliberate. Graycat wanted to observe the herald and his people just as Silkentongue did; but the Overlord could not sit unnoticed to one side to watch. She must be in full view. So she provided a distraction to draw eyes away from her.

Medley was there to be noticed.

Graycat sat down and the Gathering sat too. Medley stood at the left of the Chair in the Trustman's traditional position at the Overlord's unguarded side, to receive, if need be in his own body, any weapon directed at the Overlord.

Another fanfare sounded and the herald of the High Overlord and all his train made their entrance, to walk slowly and with great state between the lords and ladies, landholders and guildmasters up to the dais.

Near the end of the herald's procession Cricket noticed a tall man. He caught the eye because he seemed to carry a space about him. None of the others pressed close to him; it was as if his natural dignity was so great that no one cared to intrude upon him. He held himself very upright, yet moved without stiffness, gracefully. He seemed young, even though his curly black hair was receding slightly from his broad forehead. He wore a neat beard, which surprised Cricket: only the old men at Graycat's court were bearded.

The herald bowed as he stepped up on to the dais and each

of his followers did the same, Graycat acknowledging each bow with an inclination of her head.

The herald stood at an angle to the body of the Chamber, so that he could address both Graycat and the Gathering, and his retinue lined up behind him at the same angle. Cricket had an almost full face view of them. He could not see Graycat's face. She sat half turned towards the herald, looking directly at him as he spoke, for courtesy. He could see her profile only, unless she should turn to face the Gathering again.

The man Cricket was watching had turned with the rest and he could now see his face clearly. He was not handsome but far from ugly and his large brown eyes were calm and steady; his mouth seemed about to curve into a gentle smile, although in fact he did not smile but gravely fixed his gaze on Graycat.

He was the only one, Cricket thought, who did not soon let his eyes wander to Medley's gleaming splendour. It was really very funny to watch them trying not to look at her.

The herald, having glanced back to make sure that his retinue was properly lined up, bowed once more to the Gathering, all his folk bowing with him, and made as if to speak. But as he did so, Graycat turned her head to Medley and gave a tiny nod.

Medley at once stepped forward, taking all eyes from the herald's amber magnificence. 'People of the Joined Lands!' she announced. 'The Herald of the High Overlord stands before you to address you and your Overlord. Hear him!'

She stepped back again and bowed to the herald. He gave her a stiff nod, once more raised his head and took a deep breath, with a wary eye on Graycat, and began his speech with courtly formality.

'To the Overlord of the Joined Lands, to the lords, ladies, landholders, guildmasters and guildmistresses of the Joined Lands, the High Overlord sends greetings by the mouth of his Herald.'

There was a faint sigh from the Gathering, and everyone settled down for a long flowery speech. Cricket didn't listen very closely; the herald was paying compliments to all the Joined Lands, mentioning the Elder Dragons and the victory over the Westfoldermen, and spinning it all out at length.

Instead of listening, Cricket concentrated on watching the herald's people and especially the tall man he had noticed when they entered. It really was remarkable. He did not once take his eyes from Graycat. At one point she turned her head to exchange a glance with Medley as if something the herald had said amused her; then Cricket saw him smile slightly, but all the rest of the time he just gazed. The others moved, stared at Medley, coughed, looked at the Gathering, scratched, even; but he stayed still and watched Graycat.

The herald's voice changed. He was obviously coming to the end of his politenesses and the beginning of his real message. Cricket's attention snapped back to him. He heard this, all right.

'And so, to the Overlord and the folk of the Joined Lands,' said the herald, slowly and distinctly, 'is this one sent to propose a marriage between the High Overlord Skyfriend and the Lady Graycat Quicksilver, Overlord of the Joined Lands!'

CHAPTER SEVENTEEN

A great gasp of amazement went up from the Gathering. Graycat herself stiffened, then leaned back in her chair, her face blank.

Cricket knew from Dragonfriend that this meant that she was thinking hard and fast. She stayed perfectly still until the herald had finished. Then she inclined her head graciously.

'The people of the Joined Lands are sensible of the honour done them by this offer,' she said. 'It shall be considered most carefully and at once by this Gathering. Will the Herald of the High Overlord give the Gathering of the Joined Lands leave until this evening?'

She was telling him, in the politest possible way, to go, so that they could discuss the matter in – well, not in private, exactly – but without him and his long ears.

The herald bowed very low indeed; and this time, Graycat rose and bowed also. So did the entire Gathering. They all stood in breath-held silence while the herald and his folk made their way back down the steps of the dais and along the centre aisle to the great doors by which they had come in. As they went, one of them glanced back at Graycat. It was the same tall balding man that Cricket had been watching before. Then they were gone and the whole Gathering burst into speech.

Cricket saw Dragonfriend signalling him to come, so he squeezed between the folk lining the gallery and scurried down the stair into the body of the hall.

He had difficulty in reaching the dais, for most of the Gathering were on their feet and clogging the aisles as they argued, exclaimed and almost, in some cases, came to blows over the High Overlord's proposal.

Cricket wriggled, asked folks' pardon, trod on toes, begged pardon again and finally ducked down and crawled under a bench and between the legs of a large and very startled guildmaster to reach the steps to the dais.

Dragonfriend met him, grinning. 'That's one way to do it,' she remarked, 'but don't expect it to make you popular!'

Cricket made the indignant guildmaster a hasty and apologetic bow and followed Dragonfriend to the back of the dais.

Graycat had summoned all her councillors, and such of her Over-captains as were present, up on to the dais to confer with her. It was getting very crowded. Dragonfriend and Cricket slid past them to where Silkentongue stood looking worried and talking to a much younger storyteller. Cricket did not recognise her but Dragonfriend murmured, 'My cousin Fleet. She visited the High Overlord's city a few months ago.'

Fleet was shaking her head. 'No, I never was at court, you see, Storyteller; and the High Overlord is said to dislike processions and formalities. If he ever walks or rides in his city, he does so as a private gentleman, without fanfare. His folk make a point of not recognising him publicly, out of courtesy. Indeed, I may have seen him several times and not known.'

Silkentongue nodded. 'I see. Well, it can't be helped. The Overlord will want to hear all the gossip you may have gathered about the High Overlord, so get your ideas arranged and the facts sorted from the fancies. She'll probably be sending for me soon. You will come with me.'

Then he turned to Dragonfriend. 'Sisterson's daughter, tell me what you saw among the Gathering.'

Dragonfriend looked serious. 'I noticed only one oddity among the Gathering. Everyone was startled, as you would expect, when the herald made the proposal; but one person, I thought, reacted as though he had been expecting something different and had got a most unwelcome shock. I mean Lord Wolfbane, Lady Deepskill's son.'

'Yes, I saw it, too. Interesting. I shall consider this carefully. It must go no further at present.'

He looked pointedly at Cricket, who said hastily, 'I shall keep silent, Storyteller.'

He was longing to ask questions about Wolfbane. Dragonfriend had mentioned his name as an example when she spoke of candidates for the Overlordship; had he been in her mind already as a danger? What sort of man was he? How nearly was he related to the old Overlord?

But the Storyteller was speaking again. 'Let us have your report now, Cricket,' he said.

Cricket gathered his wits. 'I was watching the herald's folk as Dragonfriend told me,' he began, 'but a lot of the time I was looking at one man in particular. Dragonfriend said to look for anything out of the ordinary and – well, the others did treat him rather differently.'

He hesitated, and Silkentongue prompted him. 'Which one was he?' he asked.

Cricket described the man as exactly as he could. 'I'm sure he is someone important; but, I'm sorry, I couldn't help looking at the Overlord when the herald finally made his proposal, so I didn't see how he reacted. I'd been watching the herald's people carefully till then, really I had! But there was nothing else you could call out of the way. I mean, you'd expect them to look knowing, wouldn't you? They were just waiting for the herald to say his piece and startle us all.'

He looked anxiously at the Storyteller, and he smiled and nodded.

'So there is nothing for you, sir, not really, except the way that one man fixed all his attention on Overlord Graycat. He even looked back as they left and no one else did.'

'Ah, now I know the man you mean,' Silkentongue said. 'Yes, I noticed that one of them turned to look back. Well, now, you've not done at all badly, youngster. Don't fret yourself any more.'

He smiled kindly at Cricket and turned to Dragonfriend again. 'Did you notice this man at the banquet? I don't believe I did.'

'I think he was there,' said Dragonfriend, frowning. 'But I can't recall noticing him particularly.'

'Now that is interesting.' Silkentongue stared thoughtfully into space for a moment. 'Our Cricket may have done better than we thought. Neither of us noticed him at the banquet, but Cricket takes note of him here! Hmmm.'

Cricket had his mouth open to ask why this was important when Medley slipped through the crowd and tapped Silkentongue on the shoulder.

'The Overlord desires your advice, Storyteller,' she said softly and at once Silkentongue beckoned Fleet and Dragonfriend and went to obey the summons.

'Wait here, Cricket,' Dragonfriend said hastily. 'I don't want to have to search for you.' And then she was gone, too.

Cricket could not see Graycat, seated in her Chair of State, for all the councillors standing round her; and Fleet, Silkentongue and Dragonfriend, who were none of them tall, were swallowed up by the crowd. He could just see the top of Medley's head – the silver scarf on her piled-up hair made a good mark and she was taller than most men anyway – but she was soon sent on another errand and vanished into the body of the hall. It was no good straining to see, so he listened instead to the nearest councillors.

Farwalker's name caught his ear. A lady had said something about him and another replied briskly, 'Farwalker? Well, Starshadow, what can he do? Or even say? After all, he can never, or not since she was proclaimed the Young Overlord, have had any real hope of her, surely?'

'Not having any real hope is not quite the same as having no hope at all,' said Starshadow quietly.

'Our Lady Graycat must marry the High Overlord. He is the

best match anyone could dream of,' insisted the other.

'I do not advise you to use the word 'must' to our Overlord,' said Lady Starshadow, sounding amused. 'I seem to remember that her own father did so once, about a match he wished her to make!'

'Oh, that! When she was – how old? Seventeen? I should hope she is wiser now; besides, she can hardly run away this time!'

'Nevertheless, if you wish for this marriage, give her no reason for anger,' said Starshadow. 'I shall not mention Lord Farwalker. Do not you, either!'

The other lady made a scornful noise through her nose. 'I am not quite the fool you think me!' she snapped.

Then they moved away and Cricket had something else to worry about.

Did they mean that Graycat might refuse the marriage because she loved Farwalker? Or that Farwalker would – might – make trouble because he loved her? He looked round to see if Farwalker was anywhere near but couldn't spot him.

Cricket set himself to summon up all he knew about Farwalker and Graycat. After Graycat had fled her father's Hold to escape a forced marriage, she had lived among the actors, even becoming a member of that guild. She had lived as a peasant and as a soldier for a time, until she had been outlawed for killing a lord's son who had attacked her. In escaping, she had also killed the lord himself and several of his men.

Somewhere along the way she had met Farwalker and they had been comrades for the last four or five of the seven years of Graycat's outlawry. Farwalker had not been outlawed but because he was with Graycat he had been hunted too. Why would he have stayed with her unless he loved her? He had risked his life for her many times, not least when he had shot down Lord Freeforest in this very Chamber, to save her from Lord Freeforest's poisoned dagger.

But she had risked her life for him, too. Cricket thought of some of the stories he had heard. Graycat had once rescued Farwalker from a landholder who, illegally, had intended to hang him. She had ridden her horse straight through the landholder's men, slashed Farwalker's bonds, hauled him up behind her and galloped away. The rescue had been so reckless that the men had just stood and stared, incredulously, and let her escape unharmed.

It was hard to believe this was the same person who had just so graciously dismissed the High Overlord's herald. Was she ever reckless nowadays? Perhaps she might be about this marriage.

Dragonfriend suddenly reappeared. 'Cricket,' she said very softly, 'we've to attend the Overlord in her private rooms. It seems there is a further, secret message from the High Overlord!'

CHAPTER EIGHTEEN

'I requested a private interview, Overlord Quicksilver.' The herald was looking pointedly at Dragonfriend and Cricket.

'My name is Graycat,' replied Graycat, coldly. 'It is clear that your memory, Herald, needs prompting. My Trustman will keep the door and ensure we are not disturbed. My Remembrancer and her apprentice shall stay.'

The herald said quickly, as if scoring a point, 'If your Remembrancer's apprentice is to stay, then I wish one of my people to be present.'

Graycat looked bored. 'Of course,' she said. 'For whom shall I send?'

The herald asked for a certain Lord Cloud. Cricket wondered which of the herald's followers would appear. They had to wait several minutes. Dragonfriend and Graycat showed nothing at all, but the herald seemed nervous.

At last the door opened and the tall youngish man Cricket had noticed at the Gathering came in. He was perfectly calm and seemed not to have been hurrying himself particularly.

The herald explained why he had been sent for and Cloud bowed slightly but did not speak.

Graycat smiled at him and said, 'Please sit with my Remembrancer, friend Cloud. Now, Herald, to your real business.'

The herald said hastily, 'The marriage alliance proposal is real enough, Overlord. I beg you to credit it!'

He sounded alarmed and Graycat laughed at him, silently. It was very like the way the wolf Drinks-the-Wind sometimes laughed. It was not altogether reassuring. The herald began to sweat.

He said, rather loudly, 'First, I must have your Remembrancer's word that nothing I say here will be mentioned outside this room.'

Graycat gave him a thoughtful stare. 'And mine also?' she asked.

'I fear that what I have to say to you, you will not wish repeated beyond these walls,' said the herald ominously. 'I ask your Remembrancer's word as much for your sake as for the sake of the High Overlord.'

'You have my word,' said Dragonfriend, without waiting for Graycat's permission. The Overlord turned to stare at her, surprised, but Dragonfriend went on: 'and that of my apprentice, Cricket Storyteller. I, Storyteller Wolftalker Dragonfriend, Witness and Remembrancer to Overlord Graycat, pledge you Guild Oath that neither I nor my apprentice shall repeat one word of what is said in this room without leave from the Herald of the High Overlord or from Overlord Graycat.'

Cricket found himself making the sign against ill fortune. He felt cold and a little sick. She had given her word on his behalf. If he ever broke it, she, not he, must answer to the Guild of Storytellers. It tied his tongue even more firmly than his own oath would have.

Graycat nodded. 'My Remembrancer takes you seriously. So do I. Say on, Herald. What does the High Overlord have to tell me?'

'The High Overlord Skyfriend says: 'We have been warned against you, Young Overlord Graycat Quicksilver. We have been told that you will never be proclaimed as Overlord, that your hold upon the Joined Lands is weak and growing weaker, that the people are rising in arms against your rule and that, in order to raise money to hire mercenaries, you have agreed to the destruction of the Gilden Forest, which you and the Overlord of Westfold are jointly pledged to maintain. All these things we have on good authority, yet none of them do we believe. We beg you to show our Herald proof, if you will, that these vile rumours are false. We cannot keep the rumour mongers quiet for long. As you will know, tales of the wickedness of rulers are always popular.

"Our proposal of marriage is an honest one, yet at the same time we hope by it to balk the malice directed at you. We cannot hope to crush it altogether, so you must look to your own defences, Overlord. And, we fear, you must seek among those of your own court for your enemy.' So says my master.'

There was a pause. Graycat sat motionless. Cricket was consumed with fury and fearful suspicion.

'Wolfbane?' he mouthed at Dragonfriend and she shrugged her shoulders, looking as frightened as he felt.

Graycat said sharply: 'If you know anything of this, Cricket, speak up instead of making faces at my Storyteller.'

His heart jumped at her tone. He found he was on his feet, quite without intending it, and shaking.

'I – I beg the Overlord's pardon,' he said, tripping over the words, 'but I don't know anything at all. Not of my own knowledge.' He stopped, not knowing how to explain about his promise to Silkentongue.

Dragonfriend came to the rescue. 'Cricket only knows what I have told him. I think perhaps I should tell it to you alone, my Overlord.'

Graycat looked frowningly at her, then called to Medley to come in.

'Stay here with my guests for a little while, Blademistress,' she said. 'I have a private audience to give.'

Medley looked surprised but bowed and Graycat took Dragonfriend into the next room, shutting the door firmly behind them.

There was an awkward silence. The herald and Cloud both stared at Cricket speculatively while he tried to look unconcerned. He felt his ears getting hot, however.

Medley caught his eye and grinned. Then she began to make polite conversation with the herald, who was obliged to stop staring and answer her. Medley, Cricket discovered, could be very charming when she chose. The herald was soon thawing nicely.

Lord Cloud looked as though he wanted to laugh. Then he turned to Cricket.

'I have heard stories of Blademistress Medley,' he said softly. 'I can believe them all now. Has she any of her knives with her?'

Cricket was shocked. 'In the Overlord's presence? At court? Of course not!'

But was that true? Medley had, Cricket knew, some very small slender knives that could double as hair ornaments. Quite possibly, some of the pins holding that pile of hair in place were not pins at all... And Graycat had addressed her as 'Blademistress', not 'Trustman'...

He stared at his feet in confusion, wondering what to say.

'She is a remarkable woman,' said Cloud. He didn't seem to notice Cricket's sudden silence, 'as is your Overlord. Are you in trouble with her now?'

'Oh, no. The Overlord is never unfair,' Cricket said proudly. 'Dragonfriend will explain why I couldn't tell her about – uh...'

'About whatever it is?' Cloud smiled at him. Cricket decided not to talk any more. He found himself liking Cloud and was afraid he would let his tongue run on too freely. So he smiled back and nodded, his lips pressed firmly together.

Graycat and Dragonfriend returned, Graycat frowning, Dragonfriend looking relieved.

'My Storyteller thinks she knows who my enemy may be,' the Overlord said abruptly. 'I don't like it; but I believe she is right. There is a person, a relative of mine, who may feel – superseded – by me. He might well find pleasure in spreading rumours and manipulating events to my downfall. I can deal with him. And I shall.'

Her face was smooth, now. She even smiled a very small smile.

Cricket shivered and was glad not to be Wolfbane.

'The rumours and the events which have been set in motion are another matter,' Graycat went on. 'Your Lord seems to think that if I am known to have received his proposal and to be about to accept it, it will give pause to some of those who ill-wish me. What does he think will happen if I refuse?'

The herald looked blank. Then he glanced at Cloud and said: 'I do not know the High Overlord's mind. I only know his message. Cloud here is close to the High Overlord. Can you answer Overlord Graycat's question, Lord Cloud?'

So, Cricket thought, I was right. Cloud is someone important.

He bowed to Graycat. 'Lady, I do not think the High Overlord expected a refusal; but this might well improve your position still more. No one would believe you feared for your Overlordship if you could afford to turn down such an offer.'

Graycat flung back her head and laughed aloud. She was clearly delighted with Cloud's answer.

'Oh, wise High Overlord, to send me an honest man,' she said, still laughing. 'As to the rumours, my Storyteller is going to the Gilden Forest as soon as I have been proclaimed (and this will take place exactly as planned, I do assure you), and she will find out what is happening there. The uprisings will, I am reasonably certain, die down as soon as my enterprising young relative has been shown the error of his ways.'

She stood up. 'Herald, my Great Gathering must still discuss your master's offer; but my answer will be "Yes".'

Dragonfriend gasped and stood rigid beside Cricket.

'In the name of the High Overlord, this one thanks the Overlord of the Joined Lands for her gracious acceptance of the High Overlord's offer,' said the herald, with the utmost formality.

At that moment Cricket realised that Dragonfriend and he had just Witnessed the betrothal of Graycat Quicksilver,

103

Overlord of the Joined Lands, to Skyfriend, the High Overlord. He almost stopped breathing in shock.

He saw Medley realise it too. She looked startled, her hand going automatically to her empty belt, then relaxed and smiled, determinedly. She bowed formally to Graycat.

'May it be for the happiness of the lord and the lady and the prosperity of the Land!' she said, in the traditional words with which the marriage of a lord or overlord is greeted.

Cricket looked at Dragonfriend to know what to do or say, saw she was bowing and hastily copied her.

Graycat smiled at them then looked consideringly round the room. 'I think we have been too long absent from the Gathering,' she said. 'Sir Herald, Lord Cloud, my Trustman will escort you to your rooms. Storytellers, attend me.'

They followed her back to the High Chamber. On the way they met Farwalker, who was evidently searching for the Overlord for he looked very relieved to see them.

Graycat spoke softly into his ear and he exclaimed 'Wolfbane!' in a shocked under-voice. He bowed. 'As the Overlord wishes.'

He took the ring she held out to him and vanished towards the guards' quarters.

Cricket looked his question at Dragonfriend and she murmured, 'Who else can she trust if one so near the Overlordship must be arrested?'

Bull was waiting by the Overlord's door into the High Chamber. Medley had sent a page to fetch him, since she herself was attending the herald. Graycat hesitated. Cricket could see why. It was not proper to take a bodyguard into the Great Gathering but suppose Wolfbane should attack her when he knew he was found out?

'Stay here, Bull,' she told him, 'with the door just open. If I call, come to me. No weapons, mind.' Bull grinned. They all knew he needed no weapons.

The noise of all the folk in the hall arguing died down as soon as they saw Graycat coming back. Not everyone had noticed she had left, from the buzz of surprise which went round. She smiled, asked everyone to return to their place, and then turned to the oldest lord present and begged him to tell her the feeling of the Gathering.

His thin voice reached very few at first and everyone fell silent to hear.

Dragonfriend and Cricket were standing by Graycat's chair now. They caught a glimpse of Silkentongue, looking faintly amused, then Dragonfriend nudged Cricket and made a tiny gesture towards a slender young man with a slightly fixed smile on his handsome face, sitting close below the dais. Wolfbane? Cricket looked questioningly at her and she nodded.

Then Graycat said under her breath, not turning her head to them, 'Brat, where is my cousin Deepskill?' and Cricket remembered that Wolfbane was Lady Deepskill's son and heir.

He looked around the High Chamber. She was not sitting anywhere near her son. He looked further and further back in the body of the High Chamber but she did not seem to be anywhere there.

The old lord was still droning on and everyone listened, still and attentive. Cricket looked higher, up into the galleries; and here there was movement. The folk who had packed the galleries to watch the Gathering, the servants, the tradesmen from the City, the farm folk from beyond the walls were all being quietly and gently moved out and the guards were moving in.

He looked to the main doors; and the two Door wards were now eight. He glanced behind him and there was stealthy movement at the partly opened door of the Overlord's entrance, where Bull waited.

He swallowed nervously and looked back to the High Chamber, where the old lord was stopping at last. Graycat was thanking the old man. He had put the case for and against the marriage alliance very fairly. His mind was still keen even if his voice was feeble; except, of course, that he knew nothing of the rat gnawing at the roots of the Joined Lands. Cricket looked again at Wolfbane.

'Does anyone wish to add anything to what the lord of Riverstrand has said?' asked Graycat; and Cricket's heart gave a great thud as Wolfbane slowly stood up, his eyes fixed upon her as if she had summoned him.

She gazed back at him calmly, and murmured to Dragonfriend.

To Cricket's amazement, Dragonfriend stepped forward.

'Lord Wolfbane, son to Lady Deepskill, the daughter of Lord Armshield who was half-brother by his mother to Overlord Strongmind, will speak,' she announced and stepped back again.

The Gathering had been carefully reminded of how distant was Wolfbane's claim to the Overlordship, in terms which could appear to be no more than an introduction, a courtesy to those not often at court who might not know the young lord by sight.

Wolfbane knew what Graycat had done to him, though, and was thrown off balance. Cricket saw his expression change. His grin of anticipation vanished. He bit his lip and made as if to sit down again.

Then he changed his mind and strode to the dais steps.

CHAPTER NINETEEN

Standing halfway up the steps to the dais, Wolfbane prepared to address the Great Gathering. He had begun to speak the formal words of address: 'Lords, ladies, landholders –' when a voice from the very back of the Chamber broke in.

'You have forgotten the Overlord, Wolfbane.'

Cricket gasped in shock. It was Deepskill, her splendid robes swept back, her waist girded with a swordbelt, the sword itself bare in her hand. The Door wards were fanned out around her, warily closing in.

Graycat said sharply, 'Let the Door wards stand aside!' then gently, 'Why does Lady Deepskill come armed into this Gathering?'

'I have learned that my son is a traitor,' Deepskill said clearly. 'I do not intend to survive his shame but I will not insult the Overlord's presence.'

And she bowed to Graycat, deeply and gracefully, laying the sword on the floor at the lowest point of her bow. Then she straightened herself again, proudly.

From his vantage point Cricket could see that she was keeping her foot on the sword blade. He thought that she could probably pick it up before any of the guards could reach her.

Graycat rose to her full height. She said slowly and clearly, 'The Gathering has yet to hear from Lord Wolfbane. No man or woman may be condemned unheard. Let not the Lady Deepskill so condemn her son.'

Wolfbane was glaring from one to the other with shocked indecision. Graycat was still using the Courtly mode of speech which meant that the Gathering was still in session, even though Deepskill had tossed aside the court speech. Now, in his agitation, Wolfbane did the same.

'What do you mean?' he cried furiously to his mother. 'Who said this? How could you believe them?' He glanced back over his shoulder just as the door behind the dais opened fully and Medley walked through, slow and stately, taking all eyes with her glistening robes. She stood still for a moment, looking at Wolfbane, then strolled across to take her place at the Overlord's side. Thankfully Cricket stood back to give her room.

'Cousin Wolfbane,' said Graycat, so softly that her voice barely reached him, 'I do not wish to lose my councillor Deepskill.'

She raised her voice. 'Lord Wolfbane has leave to speak as he chooses and afterwards to depart or to stay as he chooses. None shall prevent him. He has the Overlord's word for his protection.'

A long sigh went up from the Gathering, till now frozen in horror. Medley patted her piled hair as if to be sure it was tidy. She did not take her eyes off Wolfbane for a second. And Farwalker slipped quietly into the High Chamber, behind Lady Deepskill.

Wolfbane turned to Graycat. 'How can I say what I meant to say now that my own mother has accused me of treason? I can think of nothing else. I can't believe she would turn against me like this!'

He turned back to the Gathering. 'If someone hates me enough to persuade my mother to believe such a vile lie, let him stand before me now and accuse me to my face! Who is it?'

It sounded wonderfully convincing; and Cricket began to fear that they had perhaps made a terrible mistake. He looked sideways at Dragonfriend. She had her head cocked a little to one side and was watching Wolfbane with interest.

She glanced at him and said, so softly that it was barely a breath, 'Now he'll say what a coward's trick it is,' and like an echo Wolfbane cried out passionately, 'What a cowardly trick to play upon Lady Deepskill!' and Cricket heard the hollowness behind the tone of outrage.

The Gathering did not hear it. A murmur went up and several people looked pityingly or reproachfully at Deepskill.

'I do not even know of what I am accused!' Wolfbane went on. 'Mother, you cannot have been convinced without evidence. You must tell me what I am supposed to have done!'

'I wondered if he would dare to say that,' remarked Dragonfriend very softly.

'But what can she know? How did she ever get the notion?' Cricket whispered back.

'Medley was not guarding the door while we were talking about him,' said Dragonfriend. 'We might have been overheard. Nobody mentioned his name, it's true, but...' she shrugged.

Lady Deepskill waited for the buzz that greeted Wolfbane's last appeal to die down.

'The Great Gathering acclaimed Graycat as the Young Overlord, Heir to the Joined Lands,' she said slowly. 'She was proclaimed at the Star Stones; you yourself were her Champion, Wolfbane, to challenge any who denied her right. She has been Young Overlord long enough for us all to know that the Great Gathering chose wisely. She will be a good Overlord to the Joined Lands, perhaps a great one. In two days' time she will be proclaimed Overlord of the Joined Lands at the Star Stones. But not if you have your way.

'Is it not treason to plot to undermine the authority of the Overlord? To stir up simple people with lies so that they rise in rebellion against an imagined threat? To bring about the death of the Overlord in the course of your plotting?'

'What are you talking about? The Overlord is standing before you, she isn't dead!' cried Wolfbane. 'For the Stars' sake, mother, are you mad?'

People were beginning to stand up and call out. The guards in the galleries clustered at the heads of the stairs. Farwalker made a quieting gesture at them and they came no further. Medley touched her hair again and her hand lingered and drew away reluctantly.

Graycat said calmly and clearly, 'Let there be silence,' and a hush fell at once.

'I speak of the Overlord Strongmind's death,' Deepskill said sadly. 'As, I fear, you know only too well. You do not choose your servants carefully enough, nor treat them well enough. I knew you intended to put yourself forward for the Overlordship at this Gathering.'

She broke off and addressed Graycat directly, 'Forgive me, my Overlord, for not telling you. I thought he would be laughed out of his foolishness, so I allowed it to go on.'

She turned again to Wolfbane. 'But, my son, your body servant came to me not half an hour ago to say that you were under suspicion and he was afraid to be questioned himself. He had overheard enough of your plans to know that they were treasonable.'

She stopped speaking for a moment and Wolfbane started to say something; but so did half the folk in the Chamber. His voice was drowned.

Under cover of the noise, Dragonfriend said urgently, 'Gray, we must stop her. If she goes into any more detail or mentions the Overlord's death again, anything may happen!'

'Yes,' said Graycat, 'I know.' She leaned over and spoke softly to Medley. Medley bowed and walked across to where Wolfbane still stood on the steps. The voices began to die down again as people noticed her movements.

Wolfbane turned sharply to face her, uneasy at having her at his back.

Medley smiled down at him and said politely: 'The Overlord begs Lord Wolfbane to say whether he still wishes to put himself forward as a candidate for the Overlordship.'

It was utterly unexpected. The whole Gathering fell silent and Wolfbane stared at Graycat with his mouth hanging open.

Medley gently urged him to step up on to the dais with a hand under his elbow. Her free hand touched her hair for a moment;

and Wolfbane went suddenly rigid, then began to walk stiffly over to Graycat, Medley very close beside him.

She spoke into his ear as they moved, her face turned from the Gathering and Cricket saw his eyes widen and his lips tremble. He fell to his knees before the Overlord, perhaps as much because his legs would no longer hold him as because Medley had told him to.

'Lord Wolfbane has no wish to be other than the Overlord Graycat's faithful servant.' he said in a strained, high voice. 'The choice of the Great Gathering is also his choice.'

He swallowed, licked his lips, glanced up at Graycat's impassive face and added, 'If errors have been made, they shall be amended.'

His voice shook on the last phrase and he bit his lip and had to steady himself with a hand on the floor. He looked sideways at Medley, who smiled very sweetly at him. Cricket was close enough to see the tiny knife she held. So, of course, was he.

'All errors shall certainly be amended,' said Graycat, calmly. 'But meanwhile, the Gathering has still to vote upon the proposal laid before it by the Herald of the High Overlord.'

The Gathering had forgotten all about the High Overlord. There was another explosion of chatter, under cover of which Graycat spoke to Dragonfriend. 'Go at once to Deepskill and beg her to meet me in my rooms. Get her out of here at any cost. Cricket, tell Bull he is to follow Lady Deepskill and see she does not harm herself.'

As he moved away, trying to be unobtrusive, Cricket heard her say sharply: 'Wolfbane!' and he started and got up off his knees. 'Go and sit down,' she told him. 'When the Gathering breaks up, come to my rooms. You still have my word, cousin; but Medley will be with you.'

Over his shoulder, Cricket saw Wolfbane stumble back down the steps.

Bull was still waiting at the private door. The guards there made way for Cricket and he gave Bull the message, very quietly. He did not need to be told that no one else should hear it.

The Gathering voted overwhelmingly for the marriage. Cricket had the feeling that they wanted the voting out of the way so that the Gathering might break up and they could all get down to gossiping about Wolfbane.

And Wolfbane sat slumped down in his seat, ignoring the voting and avoided by everyone. No one spoke to him, then or after the Gathering had closed. At the end, he walked slowly out, a wide space around him, all heads turning towards him. He looked at nobody.

That evening, a day of mourning was announced for the Overlord's cousin Wolfbane, who had slain himself for shame at being accused of treason.

CHAPTER TWENTY

'Shame? It was sheer spite,' Medley said scornfully next day. 'Hoped Deepskill would kill herself too, the little toad. So she might have done if Gray hadn't talked her round, saying that the shame was covered by his honourable death. Well, I am not wearing mourning for him, I can tell you!'

'Medley, you should forgive yourself for letting him get so near to Gray,' Dragonfriend, said gently. 'She wanted him to be given his chance. It was not your fault; and he wasn't armed, not until he snatched Deepskill's sword to die on.'

Medley gave her a grin which was almost a snarl and said nothing. Cricket was still worried.

'But are we sure he was guilty? Couldn't he have been too proud to answer such a shameful charge? And killed himself out of despair that even his mother believed it?'

Medley and Dragonfriend looked at him pityingly. Dragonfriend said kindly, 'You have a good heart, Cricket. But if he'd been innocent, he would certainly have told his mother so. She had, after all, shown herself ready to die for his shame. No, I'm sorry, but he was guilty.'

'And, rot him, died before we could find out just what he had been up to!' said Medley, viciously.

They were sitting under a tree in the grounds of the Great House. A little way away, seated on one of the stone benches, Graycat was talking to the herald and Cloud, with old Longwit in attendance, about the arrangements for the proclamation the next day. Dragonfriend watched the old Remembrancer shifting on the hard seat and sighed.

'He would insist on being the only Remembrancer for the

ceremony,' she remarked, 'but I can't see him so uncomfortable.'

She picked up one of the leather cushions they had brought out with them, to keep them from the still damp grass, and walked briskly over to offer it to Longwit.

'Bet you five silvers to one copper he refuses it,' said Medley.

Cricket said hastily, 'I'm not taking any bets,' and watched Longwit wave the cushion away indignantly. Graycat evidently insisted, for he rose reluctantly and allowed Dragonfriend to place the cushion and as she did so, Graycat leaned over and spoke in her ear. Dragonfriend stiffened in surprise and nodded.

When she returned, she said to Medley, 'Cricket and I have an errand. Will you bring in the cushions or shall I send a page?'

Medley looked at her curiously and Cricket wondered what had happened. Dragonfriend had spoken quite ordinarily yet Medley was alert and anxious.

'No, that's all right. I'll see to everything,' she said. Dragonfriend nodded and led Cricket away.

She took him to another part of the grounds where there was a practice field for the guards. Nobody was in sight when they stopped in the very middle of the field. Dragonfriend smiled at him.

'Never talk secrets under a tree,' she said, 'There might be someone on the other side. This is about the safest place in the City. You watch over my shoulder and I'll watch over yours. If you see anyone coming, tell me.'

Cricket gulped in amazement. These elaborate precautions were outside all his experience. What under Sun could Dragonfriend be about to tell him?

'You remember grumbling about the secrets Gray and Farwalker and I had which you were not to know?' she began. He nodded.

'Well, Gray has said I am to tell you. I asked her before, but she was not sure you could keep silent. I told her it was more dangerous to leave you to guess than to tell you. I don't know why she has changed her mind now but so it is. Listen carefully, Cricket. Have you ever heard of the Fellowship?'

'Fellowship of what?' Cricket asked, puzzled.

'Ah, then you haven't. Good. It is supposed to be a secret! The Fellowship is a sort of organisation linking up many of the poor and powerless of the land. It makes sure that if any landholder mistreats his folk, it becomes known and either there is public scandal or the Overlord, eventually, deals with it. A good many storytellers are involved, passing messages and so on; even some outlaws are members.'

'Your father, Storyteller Weaveword...?' Cricket asked, hesitantly.

'Yes. He was tortured to death in an effort to make him tell what he knew.'

'But – if the storytellers don't lie, how can they keep such a secret?'

'As my father did,' Dragonfriend said soberly. 'By staying silent.'

She paused, but Cricket had nothing to say. He was too shaken by a vision of Dragonfriend herself refusing to speak.

'I don't need to tell you that I have sworn never to tell any of the Fellowship secrets, or even that there is such a thing, without permission. Are you willing to swear the same oath before I tell you more, Cricket?'

He had seen this coming. 'Yes,' he said huskily.

He cleared his throat and said as firmly as he could: 'I, Cricket Storyteller, Broadleaf's son, swear by my Name that I will never, without leave given, speak of the Fellowship or reveal any secret of the Fellowship. May I live Nameless else.'

'I, Wolftalker Dragonfriend, bear witness,' said Dragonfriend formally.

He shuddered violently and she gave him a quick hug. 'It's all right, Cricket. No one but Gray knows you have been told and you can trust her to the stars and beyond! Now, this is the secret

Farwalker told to Gray and me: the Fellowship, or a part of it, knowing that Graycat is a member but not knowing that the old Overlord was also...'

Cricket gasped in astonishment and she nodded, 'Yes, one of our better-kept secrets, that; well, thinking that Gray is now, as it seems to them, on the side of the landholders, some of them have started a movement to undermine her before she can undermine them. Farwalker thinks that someone has stirred it up deliberately because there was no whisper of this until very recently. Otherwise, you see, it would have started as soon as she was proclaimed Heir. Presumably it was Wolfbane who began it, though how he got to know of the Fellowship I have no idea. However it happened, Wolfbane's death won't stop it.'

She paused and Cricket began to think hard.

'Suppose Gainscorn was a member; might he know enough of Wolfbane to go to him, after his own disgrace, seeking revenge?'

'Cricket! Surely not even Gainscorn would... Oh Sun and Moon! You may be right,' said Dragonfriend, appalled. 'That might account for the way he disappeared. Nobody has seen him since that day. And with the Overlord's illness and death, everyone forgot him. I wonder where he is now? I must tell Gray what we suspect. But about the Fellowship...'

'Is Medley a member?' Cricket asked, suddenly adding two and two.

Dragonfriend frowned at him. 'Now that is just the sort of question you should not ask,' she said reprovingly. 'What you don't know, you can't tell.' She looked all round again. 'There are one or two hand signs we make for recognition or to tell another member that there is Fellowship business to be done. Watch!' and she made the signs, her hands held carefully between them so that, even had there been watchers, nothing could have been seen.

He was almost sure that she had made one of them to Medley when they left her; but he could still say truthfully that he did not know.

'What is to be done about this undermining?' Cricket asked, when he had memorised the signals.

'Someone Gray trusts will be sent out,' said Dragonfriend, vaguely. 'As for us, we shall simply keep our eyes and ears open on our journey to the Gilden Forest.'

'We are still going, then?' Cricket was not quite as keen as he had been. Surely Wolfbane's death would have put an end to any plots to steal gildenwood?

'Yes, we are going. The day after tomorrow and Speedhand with us. In fact, I think we'd better go back to our room and start packing now,' Dragonfriend told him. 'We've stood out here long enough. Someone will notice us soon.'

The next day was the proclamation. It was an uncertain day, the sun breaking through the clouds at intervals after the early rain that soaked through everyone's finery on the way to the Grove of the Star Stones, where every Overlord of the Joined Lands was proclaimed.

The Grove was a long morning's ride from the City and everyone would spend the night there in the tents they carried with them, returning the next day at leisure.

Dragonfriend had decided that they two should set out for the Gilden Forest the next morning directly from the Grove, so they had their packs on the ponies. It was not unusual, for most people had changes of clothing with them, but Dragonfriend was, she said, anxious not to be noticed.

She went an odd way about it, Cricket thought. She told stories to everyone within hearing whenever the rain let up enough for folk to listen, stories and funny tales which she said her father had made up and which kept them all in fits of laughter. She made Cricket tell one or two, saying it was good experience for him. He had difficulty in making his voice carry but Dragonfriend just told him to try harder.

She told stories when they arrived, while their tents were put up, while their horses were picketed, while a meal was cooked.

'You'll have lost your voice by evening!' Cricket whispered to her over their midmeal.

She smiled blandly at him and began to tell him about how she had been ambushed on the way here for Graycat's previous proclamation as Young Overlord and how she had saved Farwalker's life by riding down the ambushers. They had been hired by the then Overlord of Westfold to kidnap her.

It was a part of the Story of 'How Spellbinder Lost her Name' that Cricket had not yet heard in detail, so he listened eagerly and forgot to protest any more.

He was startled when she told him that it had been Speedhand who had led the ambushers. So that was what Gainscorn had meant when he called Speedhand an ex-bandit. It had puzzled Cricket ever since, for the Young Swordsman was very unlike his idea of a bandit. No wonder she wanted him to go with them.

The proclamation took place just before sunset and there would be a feast afterwards. It was an exciting ceremony. It began with the Overlord's Champion challenging anyone who disputed the Overlord's claim, and then riding all round the outside of the Grove with trumpets sounding all the way.

The crowds ran with him, shouting and cheering but Dragonfriend had to stay beside Graycat and Cricket stayed too. He heard Graycat say, 'It was Wolfbane who was the Champion last time.' She sounded sad.

'Lord Lightfoot is a good choice,' Dragonfriend replied, determinedly cheerful. Then she added, with a deliberately provocative air, 'I still think you could have risked picking Farwalker as Champion.'

Graycat started to speak, stopped and said threateningly, 'Are you manipulating me, Storyteller?'

Dragonfriend giggled. 'Yes, of course!' she said, and they both laughed. Cricket saw Lady Jewel give Dragonfriend an approving glance. It was bad luck for the new Overlord to be anything but merry at the proclamation.

The rest of the ceremony passed in a dazzle of white robed Star Priests pressing round the silver and black of the Overlord's colours, level sunlight suddenly picking out the brilliant scarlets, deep crimsons, apple greens, golden yellows and blues worn by the landholders of every degree, and later, the flicker of torchlight and bonfires against the darkening sky.

Cricket was exhausted by then. But he was too excited to rest and followed Dragonfriend round the fires. They were both given food and drink by the feasters as they told stories, or laughed and leaped with the dancers as musicians struck up rival tunes.

Dragonfriend, as Cricket had warned her, was losing her voice. She told her latest audience huskily, 'No more, friends! I shan't be able to speak tomorrow.'

Her voice failed completely on the last word. She waved and moved away, miming dumbness whenever another group tried to stop her.

'I told you so!' Cricket said crossly.

She whispered, 'Yes. And now no one will expect me to be around telling stories tomorrow, will they?'

'You did it on purpose!' he discovered.

'Shh,' breathed Dragonfriend. 'Not so loud! Goodnight, apprentice, sleep well. We leave at dawn, remember.'

Cricket staggered into his tent and was asleep before he had finished unlacing his shirt.

CHAPTER TWENTY-ONE

Cricket was awoken, much too soon, by angry voices just outside the tent. He crawled to the flap and stuck his head out, blinking in the dawn light.

Lord Farwalker, Speedhand and, to his surprise, Lord Cloud, were arguing fiercely in low tones while Dragonfriend, still voiceless, tugged at first one, then the other, trying to make her whisper heard.

Cricket ducked back, ripped off his slept-in finery and scrambled into his travelling clothes faster than he had ever dressed before.

When he opened the tent flap, they were still at it but now Dragonfriend was speaking in Farwalker's ear while Speedhand told Cloud in a furious mutter that he most certainly was not wanted.

As Cricket went towards them, Medley appeared from behind the next tent with Graycat following her, looking sleepy and half annoyed, half amused.

'Lord Cloud, Medley tells me that you insist on going with my Storyteller to the Gilden Forest,' she said, tugging her cloak more tightly around her against the dawn chill.

Cloud bowed. 'Begging the Overlord's pardon but I do not insist,' he said, sounding as if he were mocking himself. 'I ask, merely. I would be most honoured to accompany the storyteller Wolftalker Dragonfriend. The High Overlord will wish to know how this adventure turns out and I think the Gilden Forest will show us the end of the story.'

'Have you the Herald's permission?' asked Graycat. 'You are one of his train.'

'Naturally, he was the first to know,' said Cloud, smiling.

Farwalker turned angrily to Graycat. 'Gray, I don't trust this man. If he goes, so do I!'

Graycat eyed them both thoughtfully. 'No, Farwalker, I can't spare you immediately,' she said slowly. 'You must be seen to escort me back to the City. But later, in a day or two, you could well leave to visit one of your landholdings; you are Lord of the Forests, after all. Though I don't believe the Gilden Forest was ever included in your lordship.'

Farwalker's frown relaxed and he laughed. 'I have a landholding, a very small one, not far from the southern edge of the Gilden Forest,' he said. 'I could overtake them in a few days, I expect.'

Dragonfriend stamped her foot. 'We must be unobtrusive,' she whispered. 'Just Speedhand and Cricket, Drinks-the-Wind and me. That's enough.'

'There's one of you already that will be noticed,' pointed out Farwalker, 'Where is the wolf, anyway?'

'Waiting, out there,' Dragonfriend jerked her head in the direction of the road to the west. 'And he is never seen at all unless he wishes to be noticed.'

She glared at Cloud and he smiled back at her.

'I have always wanted to have an adventure, Storyteller,' he said softly. 'No one has ever told a story about me.' He sighed and looked elaborately mournful.

Dragonfriend tried not to giggle, failed and shrugged. 'Oh, very well,' she said in her husky whisper. 'Come, then.'

That settled it. Speedhand still looked bothered but Cloud ignored his grim expression and went cheerfully away to fetch his pony. Marker and Baylock were already saddled and Speedhand was strapping his own pack behind his pony's saddle.

Cricket said worriedly, 'What about firstmeal? Don't we get any?'

They were, it seemed, to eat on the move. Graycat waved them goodbye, Medley nodded briefly and Farwalker said, 'See you in a week!' and they were away.

The most notable thing that happened in the first week of the journey was the way Cloud overcame all their reservations about his being of their company. By the time Farwalker's party caught up with them, Cloud was so much one of them that Cricket had a hard time remembering, out of the many secrets he was burdened with, which Cloud might know and which he must not.

Farwalker's arrival changed everything. Cricket could have sworn that Cloud, who had fitted in so well with them, was deliberately annoying and provoking Farwalker. It was very subtle and he was sure that Farwalker did not realise what Cloud was doing, not having seen him when he was intent on fitting in; but the two of them were soon at outs with each other. Dragonfriend became so exasperated that she refused to let them go with her into the villages on their way.

They had been telling stories as often as possible as they went, on the lookout for some evidence of the Fellowship's activities. So far, none had appeared and neither had they heard any mention of trouble in the Gilden Forest.

Speedhand and Cloud, of course, thought that they were only seeking news of the forest.

Dragonfriend was about ready to give up and make straight for the Gilden Forest; but she decided to call at one last village, not more than ten miles from the forest verge.

'You'll stay well away,' she told Farwalker, firmly. 'You are too well known, my lord. They'll not talk in front of you.'

'Whenever you call me 'my lord',' complained Farwalker, 'you say something I don't like.'

Dragonfriend ignored this. 'Lord Cloud, I don't trust you on your own, so you had better come with us. Yes, Speedhand,' she added hurriedly, 'you can come, too.'

They went into that village all feeling out of sorts. Speedhand was sulking, Dragonfriend was irritable, Cricket was nervous and Cloud? Cricket did not really understand Cloud at any time; he changed moods suddenly and had a very arrogant way of expecting everyone else to accommodate themselves to his humour; yet he could be charming and in the right mood was the best of company.

Now he seemed to be sunk in depression and hardly spoke.

Drinks-the-Wind was the only contented one. He had looked so miserable when Dragonfriend asked him to wait for them outside the village, that she had given in and told him to come along. Cricket was not at all sure it was wise; an awful lot of people knew that a Wildron wolf went around with the storyteller Wolftalker Dragonfriend and if she did not want to be recognised at once, he should be left behind. Of course, if anyone asked her name, he would be told the truth; but why invite it?

It was a miserable place, poor, dirty and listless.

One of the women saw them coming, picked up a clod of earth and had thrown it at them before she noticed Drinks-the-Wind. Then she gave a horrified shriek which brought men, women and children boiling out of houses and nearby fields. Dragonfriend made a small spitting sound of exasperation and, calling the wolf to her, slid from Marker's back to sit in the middle of the village street with her arm around his neck, just as she had, Cricket remembered, in his own village.

'Sit down, all of you,' she commanded. They did as she said, quickly. 'It makes you look less threatening,' she explained to Cloud, who was frowning, puzzled, 'and then the other person feels less angry.'

She was proved right almost at once. The villagers came cautiously towards them, but no more missiles were thrown and when Dragonfriend called out, 'Greetings! May the Great Star shine upon you!' as the custom was in the western parts of the Joined Lands, one of the men replied, 'May It shine on you also,' in a growl that could be taken as friendly.

Dragonfriend took it so. She got to her feet, smiling, and said: 'I am sorry that my wolf friend here frightened one of your people. He will do no harm, I promise,' and they were soon surrounded by the usual crowd of children daring each other to touch the wolf.

The man who had greeted them drew Dragonfriend aside, looking embarrassed. 'Storyteller, I am asking your pardon, but –' He hesitated, then burst out, 'You can't be telling us stories. We – we've nought to give you for them.'

He muttered the last words in shame and Dragonfriend said quickly, 'Shelter for the night for me and my companions? We have our own food. My apprentice Cricket will tell one tale or story for each of us. How will that suit you?'

'Four tales for just a night's lodging!' The man smiled for the first time. 'Generous indeed, Storyteller! Hear that, folks? The storyteller's apprentice will be telling four tales tonight!'

'Or Stories, friends. Your choice,' Cricket told them.

They ended up sharing some of their food with the children. Cricket had never seen such starveling creatures, not even in the worst winter he could remember. And this was not winter.

'Whatever has happened here?' he asked Dragonfriend when, his four tales told, they were laying out their blankets in the cottage they had been loaned. Its owner, a thin silent girl, had gone to sleep in a cousin's home.

Dragonfriend had been gossiping with some of the women, casually, making them laugh, giving them news of the rest of the Joined Lands, particularly of Graycat's proclamation, and letting them tell her such news as they would.

'Outlaws, that's what has happened,' she said in a furious under-voice. 'Oh, they didn't say so; but I could hear what they weren't saying. They seem to have taken over the whole village for months. They've been gone about twelve days, as far as I can tell, and taken everything with them that wasn't nailed down!'

'Twelve days?' Cricket said eagerly. 'That's just before Wolfbane's death. If they are the ones who are to cut down the trees, they'll not have heard.'

Speedhand said softly, 'Outlaws? So that's why none of these folk would speak to me. Do I still smell of it, Dragonfriend?'

She shook her head but he still scowled miserably. 'I'd like to get my hands on those –' he bit off what he was about to say and knelt to smooth out an invisible crease in his blanket.

Cloud sat on his, hugging his knees and said, 'One of the younger women is approachable, I think. I could persuade her to talk a little, perhaps.'

Dragonfriend shook her head. 'Too dangerous. Leave it, Cloud. Please,' she added, as Cloud raised his eyebrows in his most arrogant fashion.

'As soon as we are well away,' she promised, 'we shall send to the lord of this land for help for the people. One of Farwalker's men can go, when they reach us.'

In the middle of the night they were woken by a sudden hubbub. Speedhand was cursing as he struggled with his flint and steel to get the candle alight; and then there was a faint growl as Drinks-the-Wind pushed the door open and came in. The candlelight showed them that Cloud's bed was empty.

Dragonfriend was pulling on her clothes in frantic haste. 'That birdbrain! He's done it! I told him not to – oh, I'll send him packing, I'll – Cricket, get our gear together – no, you do it, Speedhand, Cricket and I had better go and try to…' her voice was muffled as she dragged her tunic over her head and made for the door.

Cricket followed, still trying to get his boots on, hopping ludicrously after the wolf.

Cloud was the centre of a furious group, all men. He seemed to have been hit on the head, for he appeared to be only half conscious and was muttering to himself, his Northern accent much stronger than usual.

Dragonfriend did not wait to be noticed but marched briskly over and said, clearly and coldly, 'What has this idiot done now?'

CHAPTER TWENTY-TWO

Everyone turned, startled. They saw Drinks-the-Wind pressed against Wolftalker's legs and hastily gave her room.

'If there were anything stupid to be done, I believe you'd do it, Cloud,' she went on, sounding so like Stark at her sharpest that Cricket almost looked round for the carter. She went on scolding Cloud while the villagers, bemused, tried to interrupt and explain what had happened. She would not listen... until Cloud seemed to have recovered himself somewhat.

Now Cricket understood why she was railing so. No one must question Cloud while he was half stunned and might say what he should not.

At last she allowed one of the men to get a word in.

Cloud had been caught trying, they claimed, to seduce one of the women. Wolftalker was shocked and dismayed and apologetic and, apparently, believed every word. She agreed to Cloud's being locked up in an old hut and begged to be allowed to make it up to the villagers in some way.

Cricket listened respectfully as Storyteller Wolftalker Dragonfriend wound a hostile group round her little finger.

In the end it was agreed that she should tell them a new, a fire-new, just-invented Tale, which should be known by the name of their village, Narrowvale, whenever it was told in the future. They would spend the next day in the village and tell the new tale before the lastmeal, then leave in the morning. Cloud would stay locked up until they left.

'And serve him right, bacon-brained numbskull that he is,' snapped Wolftalker, when she had explained matters to Speedhand and they had unpacked again.

'Speedhand. I think you had better leave as soon as it is properly light. Tell them you can't wait, that you have to get on. Then you can find Farwalker and tell him what has happened.'

Speedhand agreed reluctantly. Before he left, Wolftalker made some alterations to their plans.

'We shall leave tonight, as soon as we can slip away. There is to be a celebratory lastmeal after the storytelling. I couldn't get out of that; but the children will be sent to bed when they have eaten and then we shall leave. I have told Loveday, who owns this house, and she will make our farewells and apologies tomorrow morning.

'These people are so scared of the bandits that they are quite likely to warn them if they think we are suspicious about the gildentrees. That's why I want to go before they expect us to. Loveday has promised me she won't say a word until morning. I believe we can rely on her.'

Cricket was relieved. The sooner they were away from here the better. 'But what about Cloud?' he asked. 'He won't be let go till morning.'

Wolftalker said coldly: 'I am in charge here, Cricket. He disobeyed orders. As far as I am concerned, he can catch us up or go back to the City; or return to the High Overlord. Perhaps Farwalker may leave one of his men to escort that pea brain wherever he will. I've done with him! He came very near to ruining everything.'

Wolftalker spent most of the day polishing her Tale. It was, she told Cricket, one she had been thinking over for some time. She did not want him hovering, she said, so he suggested telling Cloud what they intended. Wolftalker shrugged.

'Very well. I suppose we ought to,' she said. 'But don't let anyone hear what you say. Take Drinks-the-Wind with you and sit against the wall of the hut, making as if you are talking to the wolf.'

'But Cloud can't understand the Elder tongue,' Cricket protested.

'Speak in the Common; the villagers won't know what language you are speaking if they're not near enough to hear you,' said Wolftalker impatiently.

So he did. Fortunately, the children did not find them until Cricket had given Cloud the news. He did not argue, just asked if he could get him some water as the villagers had not come near him since he had been shut in.

Horrified, Cricket fetched water and unwedged and unbolted the hut door. One of the women, warned, of course by the ever-present children, tried to stop him; he drew himself up haughtily and gave his best imitation of the Master of Pages instructing a careless lad.

'Do you really desire your village to be Named as cruel, refusing a man water?' he said coldly. 'I'll pay you for it, if you insist,' he added.

The woman looked shocked. Pay for water? The idea had never entered her head, and drove out her objections.

'Oh, if you're just giving him a drink... I thought you were letting him out,' she said, awkwardly.

Cricket gave Cloud the water and a couple of oatcakes. They had very little food left but he would not take any from the villagers.

It was not till that moment that he wondered where the food for the celebratory lastmeal was to come from. The children told him.

One of the men had gone to the next village, five miles to the south, and invited the entire village to come to hear Our Own Tale. The price of admission was to be sufficient food for both villages!

It was an admirable plot and made Cricket laugh so hard that Drinks-the-Wind was quite worried and tried to lick his face.

That evening Wolftalker gave them her full Name before she began to tell the Tale. Up till then she had told them to call her

Wolftalker, and they had not connected her with the Overlord's Storyteller Dragonfriend. The news that they had been hosting Storyteller Wolftalker Dragonfriend, Storyteller, Witness and Remembrancer to the new Overlord, who had once been Spellbinder, overawed them completely.

She had to make several jokes before they could relax enough to listen to the tale, called 'Narrowvale's Tale of the Wolf and the Fool.'

'There was once a very clever wolf,' began Wolftalker, 'who was asked by a magician to look after a stupid man who had to go on a long journey. Now the wolf did not see why he should waste his time on a man, particularly a stupid one; but the magician had once done him a great favour so, reluctantly, he agreed. The man, who was really exceptionally stupid, did not want to be looked after by a wolf and said so. The wolf, of course, could not understand the man's words but he could tell a lot from the tone and from the man's smell. His neck fur bristled and he began to growl very softly. The magician rubbed gently behind his ears, smiling.

"My dear sir,' he said, 'if you do not accept the guidance of my friend here politely, you may instead make the journey as a flea in his coat.'

'At this the wolf, who could understand the magician's words, stopped growling and grinned instead. The man did not trouble to understand the wolf but he certainly paid attention to the magician. So there they were, neither of them happy about the other but bound to try to get on together.'

The children all giggled. Wolftalker laughed with them and went on, describing the journey and the difficulties the wolf had to endure.

'The wolf found the man a terrible trial. He couldn't hunt his food, he couldn't smell anything and his hearing was poor. Indeed, the only things he seemed to do well were eating the food the wolf caught while complaining that it was not what he was used to, sleeping soundly and snoring as he slept while the wolf stayed awake to guard him.

'One day he fell into a pit someone had dug for a trap. The wolf had carefully walked around it, growling to warn his companion; but the man, too stupid to notice the wolf's warning, charged blindly across. He crashed through the branches spread to hide the pit and lay screaming for help and thrashing uselessly. The wolf tore a length of thick ivy from a nearby tree and lowered it for the man to climb out by. He held on, even though he felt as if his teeth were being pulled out, until the man was safe once more. But the man did not so much as thank him, merely grumbled at the wolf for letting him fall into the pit.'

Everyone laughed this time and Wolftalker described several more of the man's misfortunes and the wolf's cleverness in saving him.

'At last they reached the end of their journey. The wolf had never been told what the man was seeking and he did not care. He just wanted to be rid of him; so when the man suddenly said:

'There it is! There is the fountain!' he did not even wonder what fountain it was or why the man wished to reach it. He simply sat and watched the man run to the tiny jet of water and crouch down.

The man drank deeply. Then he stood up and gazed around him as if he had never properly seen anything in his life before. He listened as if he had been half deaf all his life. Then he began to touch leaves and flowers and stones as if he had never before known what it was to touch anything; and he sniffed the air and smelled the flowers and suddenly he began to run and leap into the air for joy.

'He came back to the puzzled wolf, panting and laughing, and begged the wolf to forgive him for his bad manners and ingratitude on their journey.

"This,' he told the wolf, 'is the Fountain of Knowing. It makes you understand things as they really are; and now I see how stupid I have been. I am no cleverer than before, but now that I know what I am, I mean to make the best of myself. May I hope for your company on the journey home? I will follow you and try to learn from you.'

'The wolf listened carefully to the man's voice and liked the new tone he heard in it. He waved his tail, very gently took the man's sleeve in his teeth and led him a few paces back the way they had come, to show him that he agreed. Thus they returned to the magician, each trying hard to understand the other. On the journey they became such good friends that when they arrived the wolf told the magician that he would like to go on taking care of the man, while the man said that he could not manage without the wolf. So it was that these two lived together for the rest of their lives in great contentment.'

As soon as she finished there was a great storm of applause; and then Wolftalker was begged to tell the tale again, so that the villagers might remember it better. She glanced at the setting sun, hid her impatience and began again, as if nothing could please her more.

The feast was as great a success as the tale. After it, most of the children had to be carried away to bed. Wolftalker and Cricket helped with several. Finally, they carried Loveday's youngest cousins home and simply kept going, past her cottage, where they picked up their packs, their saddles and bridles, to the field beyond where their ponies had been tethered.

They saddled and bridled Marker and Baylock and led them softly out of the field. Cloud's pony brought Cricket's heart into his gullet by whinnying loudly after them, but nobody seemed to notice.

They rode quietly away in the darkness to rejoin Farwalker.

CHAPTER TWENTY-THREE

They found Farwalker waiting for them about a mile up the road. He told them that he would himself set Cloud on his way next morning.

'And I'll make sure that his way is not ours any longer,' he said grimly.

'Don't quarrel with him,' begged Dragonfriend. 'Please, Farwalker! He really has been punished quite enough. He's been hit over the head, left without any food or drink save the water and oatcakes that Cricket took him, and now he's been abandoned. He'll hardly want this story told about him, either!'

Farwalker looked coldly at her. 'He endangered you and your companions,' he said flatly; and Dragonfriend turned away, her shoulders drooping.

They had to ride a couple of miles further before they reached the camp Farwalker's men had set up. Speedhand greeted them cheerfully. Dragonfriend smiled at him but wouldn't talk much.

Dragonfriend and Cricket had their own fire at a little distance from them all. She was very quiet and he was worried enough to pluck up his courage and ask her what was troubling her.

'I once made a promise to Bowyer Heartwood that I would try to stop Farwalker's rages,' she said, sadly. 'When he is really angry, he does not care what he does. I think he hardly knows. Heartwood can divert him and stop the fury and so can Gray; but Heartwood is very old and Gray... Well, at the time when I made the promise, I thought Farwalker and Gray would marry. That was before she was made the Young Overlord, of course. And now she is to marry the High Overlord... So it is up to me now and I can't do it.'

'You'll have to marry him yourself,' Cricket said, trying to joke her out of her gloom. To his dismay she took him seriously.

'That is what Heartwood wants,' she said. 'He believes I can influence Farwalker.' She spoke in an almost indifferent tone, staring into their tiny fire; and Cricket was startled to see that she was blinking away tears.

'It's not possible, of course,' she added, still calmly. 'When he looks at me, he doesn't see me. He sees Brat, the child he had to look after. Do you know, he almost always calls me Brat. He hasn't noticed that I've grown up.' She rubbed her eyes hastily on the back of her wrist.

'Do you mean you want to marry him?' Cricket asked, astonished.

Dragonfriend turned on him fiercely. 'I've wanted to since – oh, practically since I met him! Only – he and Gray – you don't understand, how should you...' She blew her nose and glared at Cricket as if the whole thing were somehow his fault.

Cricket thought of his eldest sister, who had married a neighbour's son with the utmost calm. It had all been arranged tidily and sensibly and she was placidly happy. He was baffled by Dragonfriend's misery.

'You were awfully young then,' he said uncertainly. 'Are you sure you won't change your mind? He's quite old, really...'

He trailed off, afraid of blundering and saying something hurtful. To his surprise, she laughed. It wasn't much of a laugh but better than crying.

'Do you think I haven't told myself all that a hundred times? And besides, I know that he ought to marry some lord's daughter; then he'd have 'influential connections', and his children would be lords and ladies by birth and acceptable to the landholders as he is not; except that he doesn't care about any of that.'

She poked a stick into the flames. 'He cares about Gray and about the Joined Lands and about being the Archer. He'd never come to Court at all if he didn't have to and if it weren't for Gray.

I truly believe he would have refused the Lordship of Freeforest when the old Overlord bestowed it on him if he hadn't been so amazed. Gray pushed him into accepting; and it would have been very ungracious to refuse. Almost impossible, really.'

'So what do we do about Cloud?' Cricket asked, hoping to change her mood.

'Hope that Farwalker has recovered his temper by morning. There's nothing more we can do.' She shrugged. 'We must go on as fast as we can at first light. I have a very fair idea of the way those outlaws went and we should come upon some trace of them. I mean us to go on by ourselves, Cricket; just you and me and Drinks-the-Wind. Farwalker's people will obey me and wait here for him, I believe. Speedhand – well, he'll be more difficult. I think I shall ask him to stay to see that Cloud is all right. Cloud is my responsibility still. Yes, I know I said I had done with him, but I was angry and not thinking. I can't abandon him entirely.'

Dragonfriend was right both times. Farwalker's people, in their lord's absence, obeyed her and stayed in their camp when the others left. And Speedhand was indeed more difficult. He flatly refused to leave them. Nothing Dragonfriend could say would move him. He had his orders from Overlord Graycat; he would obey them.

The four of them travelled fast and did not stop all day. When it grew dark and the ponies were too tired to go further, they stopped, lit a fire and began to get a meal ready.

Drinks-the-Wind had vanished, hunting his own food, and Speedhand had taken their waterskins to fill them at a nearby brook when a sour-faced and vinegar-voiced farmer appeared out of the dusk and announced that he wanted no wanderers camping on his fields.

Dragonfriend tilted her head in that unconsciously proud storyteller way and replied politely that they had no intention of setting foot on his fields. The roadside was free, as was the thicket where they had built their fire. Her voice was gentle; but

Cricket could hear the anger beneath the calm.

The man peered at her. He may not have seen the storyteller blue of her scarf in the dim light... Likely he would not have cared if he had.

'You be telling your master what I am saying,' he said. 'I'm not arguing with sluts,' spat at her feet, turned and made off. Dragonfriend did not move but Cricket ran a few steps after him, filled with rage.

'May you eat earth!' he yelled the Farmer's Curse after him. In a famine, the starving did sometimes eat the very soil to try to quiet their bellies. Hardly had he got the last word out when Dragonfriend's hand slapped across his mouth, silencing him.

'You are a storyteller! Your words have force and meaning! You may not misuse them.'

He stood gaping at her, bemused. She had turned on him now!

'Would you curse the crops?' she demanded, waving at the fields beside the road. 'Is it your desire to see little children starving? Be silent until I give you leave to speak!'

He was silent indeed, from pure amazement. Then he began to be angry. Why should she speak to him like that and for nothing?

Or almost nothing. No one that Cricket had heard of had ever been harmed by that curse; it was just about the worst thing you could say to another farmer, of course; but it was only words, breath, air – nothing!

He glared at Dragonfriend and opened his mouth to tell her how stupid he thought her to lose her temper for so small a thing.

And he could not. Nothing came out. His voice was gone.

Cricket began to shiver. All his anger slipped away. He clutched his arms around himself and clenched his jaws to stop his teeth chattering. What had she done to him? He could not even ask her!

Speedhand had just got back with the water and Dragonfriend turned away to tell him of the farmer's visit. Cricket wanted to scream at her for behaving as if nothing was the matter when she had punished him so terribly.

What would become of him, a storyteller with no voice?

The fear and self-pity swelled and grew. Cricket crept back to the ponies and buried his face in Baylock's mane. He told himself that he had done no harm. What force could the words of a mere apprentice have? Dragonfriend was cruel to behave as if his words had the same power as her own. Perhaps she did not realise that he, not being a storyteller born, could not do what she did?

Tears leaked out of his eyes. Then the pony tossed his head, nearly hitting his nose and Cricket hastily jerked back, turning to see what had disturbed him.

Dragonfriend stood beside him, looking worried.

'Cricket?' she said in a puzzled voice. 'I didn't mean to upset you so. It's all right. You've done no real harm. Come and have some food.'

She half turned, paused and turned back to look at him more closely. Cricket had flattened himself against the pony's side and was shaking his head miserably.

'Whatever is the matter with you? Cricket! Tell me!' and Cricket's throat loosened and he could speak again.

'You – you told me to be silent!' he accused her, gasping.

'Well, you needn't sulk about it,' Dragonfriend retorted, a little irritated.

'But I *couldn't* speak – I was dumb!'

Dragonfriend looked completely bewildered. She shook her head a little, as if to clear it.

'Cricket,' she said, slowly and carefully, 'You are imagining things. I am sorry I snapped at you. Now let us forget it.'

But how could he? 'I'm not imagining it,' he said obstinately. 'And if you don't believe that your own words come true, why should you try to stop me finishing the curse?'

Dragonfriend shut her eyes and sighed. Then she opened them and, with a sort of strained patience, said: 'People believe that a storyteller's words have power. Therefore they do have power, of a sort. The belief of the person who is listening is what gives them power, nothing else. Truly, Cricket, that is all it is. It is not real.'

'I felt it. It was real enough,' he told her. He was growing angry again.

Dragonfriend stared at him and went very pale. 'You really mean that you could not speak? You are not joking? But…'

She sat down plump on the roadside, shaking her head as if she had forgotten how to stop.

'No. No, I don't believe it. It isn't so; it can't be. You must be mistaken, Cricket. I can't bespell people, really I can't.'

'And what of the time you sleep-spelled a sentry? And Named Lord Eaglon into nothing? And,' Cricket finished daringly, 'Summoned the Three Elder Dragons?'

'But that wasn't – I didn't – Oh!' said Dragonfriend in exasperation. She jumped up, took two paces away, came back and sat down again, saying grimly, 'Now, listen, Cricket. Sit here beside me. We'll get this straight and then let's have no more silliness.'

He sat cautiously down and prepared to listen.

CHAPTER TWENTY-FOUR

Dragonfriend clasped her hands tightly together. She stared at them, then unclenched them and laid them in her lap as if preparing to tell a Story.

'Now!' she said, 'Let's t-take your ideas in order, sensibly. Firstly, as to sleep-spelling; you heard about that in the story of 'The Prophecy Fulfilled', didn't you?'

He nodded.

'Then you remember how Graycat was kidnapped and imprisoned by Lord Freeforest, because he believed that he could force her to marry him so that he might seize her inheritance? Farwalker was sure that Freeforest had her, but not certain where. We thought she was in his TownHold, in the dungeons. In order to find out and to get me into the airshafts leading to the dungeons, we had to go past a sentry.

'At first Farwalker thought he would have to kill the man. He did not want to. Neither did he want to leave a corpse to betray us or rouse suspicion by the sentry's disappearance. You see the difficulty? Very well, then. Now, it was a hot, drowsy day and the hottest part of the day. The man was dozing at his post. I told Farwalker and the others that I would sing the dragonsleep spell from the Story of the Last Sorceress and that it would keep the man asleep till we had finished. Bull had to have time to remove the grille over the shaft entrance to let me in and so fasten it that I could get out again later.'

Dragonfriend paused then and gripped Cricket's wrist fiercely. He jumped nervously and she glared at him. 'Listen, will you! Yes, I sang the spellsong and, yes, the sentry slept and went on sleeping while I crawled into the shaft and Medley, Shrimp,

Stark and Farwalker kept watch; and he was sleeping still when Bull replaced the grille and they all crept away in safety. But, Cricket! That sentry may well have been sleeping naturally all along. At the time I was not sure and I still am not certain that I really did anything more than convince the others they were safe. And the longer I think about it, the more I believe that that is all I did. I have never asked the others what they think. I know Bull believes in the spell; he never treads on my shadow!'

She tried to laugh; and broke off, swallowing hard. 'How would you like to be treated as a witch, Cricket? It is not pleasant, you know.'

Before he could say anything, she went on in a rush, 'As for Lord Eaglon, he had been destroyed before I Named him. Once the story of how he had murdered my father got about, he was finished and he knew it. When he came to Court no one would speak to him; his men at arms were ready to leave him at the first excuse, and did! Why, his own groom walked out when Lord Eaglon struck him for some fault. One way and another, there was really very little left for Eaglon.'

'So why Name him?' Cricket asked, cautiously.

'I didn't intend to! I was speaking to the Overlord Strongmind when I said that Eaglon was Nothing. I didn't realise that I had Named him. Well, it was not even a public audience! Only Graycat and Silkentongue were there.'

Only! Only the Young Overlord! Only the Storyteller of the Joined Lands! Had she really thought it private?

'He became what you Named him,' Cricket pointed out.

'Yes; but, Cricket, he would have become a nothing in any case! If no one will speak to you or serve you except with scorn and disdain, what sort of life is left to you? Perhaps my Naming him hastened his falling apart a little, but I did no more than that, I'm positive. He's dead now, so we can't ask him,' she finished.

'And the Dragons?' Cricket said softly.

'The Dragons! Well, no one else has tried to summon them, so how do we know that only I can?' demanded Dragonfriend crossly. 'The False Dragonmaster did it, didn't he? And they came to his summons. Yes, I know he died but the Dragons didn't kill him; it was his own fear, that's all. I believe that anyone willing to call the Three Elder Dragons with the proper words can summon them. It isn't anything special to me.'

'Anyone brave enough,' said Cricket.

'I'm a coward,' said Dragonfriend, flatly. She got up and walked away towards the fire, where Speedhand was making soup. 'And I'm hungry,' she called over her shoulder. 'Come on, Cricket, the food's waiting.'

He could not leave it alone. He ran after her and caught at her sleeve. 'What about your cursing the Westfolder Overlord and his lords?' he demanded triumphantly. 'He's dead, isn't he? And his lords. Some of them, anyway.'

Dragonfriend turned, slowly, rigidly. Her expression frightened Cricket before it smoothed out. She looked blankly at his hand and he hastily released her. He also took an unintended step back, then set his teeth and stood his ground.

'The way Gainscorn told it,' Cricket said, as steadily as he could, 'You cursed Overlord Arrow when he told you to summon the Dragons. Isn't it true?'

Dragonfriend nodded. 'It's true.' she said, dully. 'I lost my temper. I had just seen what he had done to his Court Storyteller. Now, let us –' she broke off and suddenly put both hands over her face. 'Go away, Cricket,' she muttered. 'Please!'

He went.

Wolftalker hardly spoke to him next day. Speedhand did not notice, as they were again moving fast. Cricket noticed, though, and felt miserable and ashamed. But still he stuck to it in his own mind: she had silenced him, whether she would admit it or no. And as they rode, a distant memory came back to him.

When he was very young he had crept from his bed to listen

to the story Spring Rain was telling the grownups, a story about the Last Sorceress, the Lady Dragonfriend. She had, so Spring Rain said, been able to make anyone do as she wished by the power of her speech alone. It was not a spell but a natural ability. It was called simply, The Voice. There had been some famous storytellers who had also had this gift, but who they were Cricket had never learnt, for his mother had caught him at this point and sent him back to bed. This, then was what Wolftalker had used on him; though she did not know what she had done and, hating magic as she did, refused to believe in her gift. Cricket knew that he dared not reopen the subject.

Late in the afternoon, the wolf, who had been ranging ahead, came back to them whining anxiously. Wolftalker at once pulled up and dismounted.

'Something is wrong! Show us the way, cousin,' she said.

Nervously alert, they followed the wolf through the trees. A man, a Wilder, lay bound and unconscious in the bracken. By the look of him, he had been there some time.

Wolftalker took one look and exclaimed in horror, 'I know him! That's Sings-by-Night! What has happened to him?'

'Met those starlost outlaws, I should think,' said Speedhand, grimly. He took charge at once, cutting the ropes, dribbling water into the man's slack mouth and directing the others to set up camp, get a fire going and make some broth. They did as he told them; but Drinks-the-Wind kept getting in the way, butting at Wolftalker and trying to persuade her to follow him.

At last, when Speedhand was satisfied with their efforts, she said to him, 'I must see what is the matter with Drinks-the-Wind. There may be another prisoner nearby. Can you and Cricket manage now?'

Speedhand hesitated. 'You shouldn't go alone,' he said, 'but I can't leave this poor fellow. Take Cricket.'

'I'm not alone with Drinks-the-Wind,' pointed out Wolftalker. Cricket gazed hopefully at her and she suddenly smiled at him.

'Oh, very well, you can come.'

The wolf led them deeper into the thickets. They had not gone far when Wolftalker said: 'These are gildentrees! Look, Cricket, how tall they are and how graceful!'

He looked up and promptly stumbled over a dead branch in his path. When he stopped hopping around clutching a painfully stubbed toe, he saw that Wolftalker was examining the branch closely.

'This is gildenwood,' she said slowly, 'and it has been cut. It did not fall naturally.' She looked around her carefully. 'I think the tree from which this came must have been felled here. The branches would have been lopped from the trunk to make it easier to transport and this one must have been overlooked when the rest were gathered up. Can you see any obvious gaps, Cricket?'

He stared round in his turn. The light was fading but he could still see well enough.

'Look,' he said eagerly, 'That bush over there – it's crushed and withered.'

They found the tree stump under the bush. Someone had tried to hide the evidence by uprooting a bush and planting it over the raw stump. There were chips lying around, too, left from the axe work. Wolftalker picked up one of them.

'Could anyone tell from a chip what sort of axe was used, do you suppose?' she asked. Cricket had no idea, but they both peered carefully at the stump and the chips.

Drinks-the-Wind had found some sort of trail and vanished into a tangle of thorn bushes too close for them to follow. Cricket saw him go from the corner of his eye, but was too absorbed to mention it to Wolftalker.

They moved on, found another disguised tree stump, then another. 'I fear the rumours were all too true,' Wolftalker said sadly. 'Let's go back and tell Speedhand.'

Cricket turned; and had time for no more than a horrified

gasp before his arms were seized and wrenched behind his back. He heard Wolftalker behind him cry out the wolf's name, then the sound of a blow.

Furiously ignoring the pain in his pinioned arms, Cricket twisted round to see a big hairy man. He and Wolftalker stood glaring at each other. Another man stood beyond them, with a wound crossbow, the quarrel pointed at Wolftalker.

The hairy man grinned through his beard. 'Well, now, who have we here, I wonder?' he said gloatingly.

CHAPTER TWENTY-FIVE

There was a slight rustle from beyond the thorn bushes. The wolf? But he mustn't be let to face that crossbow! Wolftalker flung the woodchip she had been clutching far out into the treeshadow, calling, 'Catch, Drinks-the-Wind!' in the Elder tongue.

Then, still looking the one who was clearly the leader in the eye, she lowered her voice slightly and said, again in the Elder tongue, 'Drinks-the-Wind, go. Seek your cousins. Seek Oakshadow. Bring cousins. Go!'

'She's casting a spell! Stop her, quick!' exclaimed the tall man who was holding Cricket.

'I have cast no spell,' Wolftalker contradicted him coldly, not even turning her head. 'Nor shall I. You have the word of a Storyteller.'

Cricket groaned silently. That meant that now she could not, even if she believed in the possibility, use The Voice on these men to free them.

'Then what were you saying?' demanded the leader, suspiciously.

'I may perhaps tell you later.' Wolftalker was still cold and a little contemptuous. 'Are you as superstitious as your friend?'

The hairy man's face twitched but he said, 'No, of course I'm not. I asked you a question, girl.'

'And I answered it,' replied Storyteller Wolftalker Dragonfriend evenly.

'Do you know what she said?' demanded the hairy man, suddenly looming over Cricket. He had never before wanted so desperately to lie. But he was a storyteller now. He nodded, clenching his teeth and hoping he looked as calm as Wolftalker.

'Then tell me!' he gripped Cricket's arm painfully.

'Not now, apprentice,' said Wolftalker, impatiently, as though he were delaying her. 'First I must deliver my message.'

'Message? How can you have a message for me?' The leader let go of Cricket and swung round on Wolftalker. 'I've heard of storyteller tricks, girl. Don't you try them on me, that's all! Don't you try anything or I'll cut your throat clean as a whistle!'

'Stars above, man – she's a storyteller! They both are!' the tall man cried in alarm. 'You can't go cutting a storyteller's throat. Let them go; or keep them till we're clear and leave them some place they'll be found later. But you can't kill them!'

Cricket saw the crossbowman nod agreement. The leader glanced across at him, then stared hard at Wolftalker, narrowing his eyes in a way which was clearly meant to be sinister. Cricket found himself wondering if the man practised it regularly and felt a silly giggle rising in the back of his throat. He bit the inside of his cheek to stop it.

There was a pause. Wolftalker looked totally unimpressed and even a little bored but the other men shifted nervously and peered at their leader sidelong.

At last he said, blusteringly, 'Well, go on, tell us this message, then. What are you waiting for? The Sky Folk to return?' and laughed uneasily.

'My message is this,' Wolftalker said composedly. 'You are in grave danger. If you fell any more trees your lives will answer for it. Even now it may be too late to save your neck.'

Then Cricket got the worst shock yet.

'Don't let her bluff you, Crusher,' said a sneering voice, a voice Cricket knew only too well. He twisted round to look; and he was right.

It was Gainscorn! He who had once been Gaingold. He stared at them with a queer smile, as if he could not believe his luck, then bent to the leader's ear and whispered.

Crusher frowned. 'Are you sure?' he demanded and Gainscorn nodded, smiling his thin smile.

'Certain,' he said, flatly.

The leader turned his scowl upon the tall thin ragged man who had grabbed Cricket.

'You two take them back to the night camp and don't let them talk. The girl will talk you into treachery if you let her. Not one word, understand? Or I'll see your guts!'

He sounded as if he meant it and their captors were clearly convinced.

The tall man assured him fervently that the prisoners should be gagged if necessary and they were dragged away.

Wolftalker risked a quick grin at Cricket and nodded to where Drinks-the-Wind had been. He grinned back, hopefully.

What could Gainscorn be doing with this scruffy band of outlaws? Cricket occupied his mind with the problem while trying to ignore the discomfort of their journey.

It was not very long, luckily. They were thrust to the ground near a fire by a lean-to hut and their feet were tied together and to each other's. Then the silent man tied Cricket's left wrist to one tree and Wolftalker's to another, so that although each had a hand free, neither could reach the other's tether nor their own feet. It was very neat and Cricket hated it.

Wolftalker, however, said admiringly, 'That's clever! And are we to be fed?'

The tall man shifted uneasily. 'He said not to let you talk,' he reminded her. 'He said you'd talk anyone into anything. Like my ma used to say, you're one as could sell slippers to snakes.'

Wolftalker pounced delightedly on the phrase. 'Did your mother make it up? Or is it a common saying where you come from? May I use it? A lovely saying, isn't it, Cricket?'

The man was gaping at her. 'You're not to talk!' he protested.

'No? Well, do at least tell me if your mother made up the saying,' urged Wolftalker. 'One who'd sell slippers to snakes!' she repeated with relish.

'One as could,' corrected the tall man.

'Yes, "could" of course,' agreed Wolftalker. 'Had your mother any other sayings?'

'I don't rightly remember.' The tall man had unconsciously relaxed and now was leaning back against the tree trunk. 'She said that about selling slippers to snakes one time when my sister tried to coax Da into letting her have a pet lamb. It stuck in my mind, kind of.'

'It would, indeed.' Wolftalker smiled at him. 'So you think perhaps she made it up on the spur of the moment?'

'Never heard nobody else use it, so maybe she did,' said the man, sounding pleased.

'I suppose I'd better not ask her name,' said Wolftalker regretfully. 'I'll have to say 'as a man I know says' when I use it.'

'Not use her name? Why not?' The tall man leaned forward indignantly.

'Well, you won't want to be identified, will you? If I use her name, someone might hear me who knows yours,' Wolftalker pointed out.

'My mother's name is Wakerobin Healer of Longview village in the Seaward Hills; and mine is Skyhigh Wanderer,' snapped the tall man defiantly. He glared at them as if they had both insulted him.

Wolftalker bowed acknowledgment. It looked a little odd, since she was sitting on the ground with her left hand tied out to the side but somehow she made it seem stately.

'My friend here is Cricket Storyteller,' she said gravely, 'and I am Storyteller Wolftalker Dragonfriend.'

There was a startled pause. Then the other man silently pulled out his belt knife, walked round to their feet and sliced through their bonds. Still without a word, he did the same for their hands. They sat and rubbed their wrists. Cricket wanted to get up and run or at least be on his feet ready, but Wolftalker did not move and he knew that he must follow her lead.

She looked up and thanked the man who had freed them so

Cricket hastily did the same. Left to himself, he didn't think he would have said thank you. He still felt too resentful at being manhandled.

It was darker now. The fire glowed more brightly and the sky was deepest blue, the stars beginning to prickle. They sat quiet until Skyhigh said slowly: 'So that's why he didn't want you to talk.'

'It is most certain,' said Wolftalker. Cricket tensed. Something was going to happen. With a great effort he held himself still and listened.

'Is it now your intent to let us go free, Skyhigh Wanderer?'

It was the other man who answered. It was the first time he had spoken.

'You are free, Storyteller. Rest here this night, and come morning we'll escort you to the road.' He hesitated and added, 'You won't remember me; but your Graycat once bound up my head.'

'I remember you,' Wolftalker told him. 'Do you still call yourself Head?'

The man grinned, embarrassed. 'It's not everyone gets Named by the Young Overlord,' he said. 'I didn't know you, Storyteller. I'm sorry. I barely saw you, that time on the road, you see. And you've changed.'

Skyhigh snorted and Wolftalker turned to him.

'Do you also mean to let us go, Skyhigh?' she asked again.

'Yes, yes, a'course,' Skyhigh hastily agreed.

CHAPTER TWENTY-SIX

Wolftalker let out a long breath. 'Now I shall tell you what I would not speak of before.'

She moved forward into the firelight, her eyes glinting, to study their startled expressions.

'I sent my cousin for help when you caught us. The Wilders should be here at any moment. By freeing us, you have saved your necks, my friends.'

'But – your cousin? There weren't no one else there!' protested Skyhigh.

'My cousin, the Wildron wolf Drinks-the-Wind, was there,' replied Wolftalker. 'Have you so soon forgotten my name? I am Wolftalker to the Wilders, and they call the wolves their cousins.'

'Magic?' asked Skyhigh, shakily. 'You can really talk to wolves?'

Both men looked nervously about them but only Cricket saw the long grey muzzle and pricked ears of a wolf, for only he had kept from looking at the flames so as to keep his night sight.

Wolftalker said calmly, 'No, not magic. Simply, the Wildron wolves are more intelligent than most. They understand some things, just as dogs can learn commands spoken to them. One does not, however,' she added warningly, 'command a wolf.'

She turned her head as she spoke and said, in the Elder tongue, 'All is well, Drinks-the-Wind.'

She rose, beckoning to Cricket and, as he scrambled up, she added in the Common speech, 'We go now, friends. If you wish to come too, you shall be welcome.'

They got to their feet, staring at her.

'My friends are here,' explained Wolftalker. 'Do you go with us?'

Then, just as they'd won, everything went wrong. Drinks-the-Wind gave a terrible snarl and sprang out of the bush, hurling himself against Wolftalker who fell sideways against Skyhigh. An arrow whipped through the space she had just left and Head gave a furious yell and charged straight through the fire, scattering the embers in all directions. There was a loud crash as he evidently collided with someone and Skyhigh, hauling Wolftalker to her feet, fled with her into the shadows behind them. Cricket dithered for a fatal moment, uncertain which way to run.

Then a huge hand gripped the back of his neck and Crusher's voice growled in his ear: 'Call off your wolf or I stick this knife into your eye!'

Drinks-the-Wind, his teeth bared, stood over a prostrate Gainscorn, snarling savagely and the furious thrashing in the undergrowth beyond suddenly ceased.

Cricket could not speak for the moment and Crusher shook him viciously.

'Call it off!' he hissed. 'And look sharp about it!'

Cricket found his voice then and said shakily, in the Elder tongue, 'Please, friend Drinks-the-Wind, let him go!'

With a last snarl Drinks-the-Wind leaped backward out of the remaining fireglow and vanished. Gainscorn stood up slowly and carefully, holding his left hand tightly in his right.

'Not an altogether successful operation,' he said calmly. 'I rather think Head got away, too.' He moved into the bushes to search.

Crusher stood motionless, still holding his dagger very close to Cricket's eye till Gainscorn returned to say: 'As I thought. One dead, one injured and no sign of Head; nor, of course, of Skyhigh and the girl. What now, great leader?'

Crusher ignored the sneer. 'Think they are still out there? The Wilders?' he asked.

'If not, their wolves will be,' said Gainscorn. 'But I'd expect one of them, at least, to be within earshot.'

'Right!' Crusher raised his voice. 'You out there! We're moving and if you value this wretched boy's life, you'll let us go and no tricks!'

'I keep telling you,' Gainscorn said resignedly, 'they don't speak the Common tongue. Let me tell them.'

Crusher looked at him suspiciously. 'Go ahead,' he said reluctantly. 'You, boy, you tell me if he says anything different.'

Gainscorn sighed patiently and repeated Crusher's words in the Elder tongue, his trained storyteller's voice carrying further and more clearly than the outlaw's. There was a distant call in reply.

'What did they say? Boy, what did the Treeboys say?' demanded Crusher.

'Just, "very well",' Cricket gasped, 'And – and then called to the wolves.' But he did not tell him just what they had called.

Gainscorn shot him a look of sardonic amusement but to Cricket's surprise, he said nothing. He knew very well that the wolves had been asked to follow them, yet he merely moved back into the bushes to help the wounded man to his feet. They set off for the outlaws' base, that dagger still far too close to Cricket's eye for comfort.

There were ten more men in the base camp, which they reached about midnight. Cricket was tired out by that time and tumbled gratefully to the ground as soon as he was given leave. He slept.

He was woken by a sharp pain in his ribs. He cried out, startled, and was answered by a grim chuckle from Crusher. It was broad daylight and Cricket was stiff and bruised from sleeping on the ground. Someone had thrown a cloak over him as he slept and he felt grateful. He looked round at the men grouped in front of him, wondering which one had bothered, and caught Gainscorn's eye. He was staring at Cricket with a peculiar expression. Cricket could not make it out; was he trying to warn him about something? What?

Cricket looked back at Crusher and some impulse made him get to his feet and say, 'Good morning,' as politely as he could.

Everyone laughed heartily. Cricket glanced at Gainscorn and he nodded approvingly. Cricket was more and more puzzled by his behaviour. First he had not given him away about the Wilders' call to their wolves and now he seemed to be keen for him to make a good impression on the outlaws. Cricket had thought that Gainscorn hated him even more than he hated Wolftalker. It made no sense.

'Not a very good morning for you, young fellow,' said Crusher with a false heartiness which sent warning shivers down his spine. 'What do you think your friends are doing now, eh?'

Cricket had no idea and said so.

A rather fat man with a straggly beard pushed forward and said eagerly, 'Let's make him tell, Crusher!' He giggled foolishly and Cricket clenched his hands to hide their sudden quivering.

Crusher backhanded the giggler casually across the face, so hard that he staggered backward, tripped on a tuft of grass and sat down with a thud.

'That's a storyteller, Handy,' Crusher said. 'They don't lie. Now keep your yap quiet.'

'We're besieged,' Gainscorn told Cricket. 'The Wilders are out there,' he waved beyond the thicket which sheltered the camp, 'and although they use no weapons, there are enough of them to overrun us so long as they don't mind taking plenty of casualties. And the wolves, of course, have their full armament with them as always.' He seemed faintly amused.

Crusher scowled. Then he bared his teeth at Cricket in a grin. Cricket would have preferred the scowl. 'But then, you see, we have you, laddie. Your girlfriend would've made a better hostage, but you'll do. They know we've got you so they're holding off. I daresay the great Storyteller Wolftalker Dragonfriend won't let them attack us, hey? What do you think?'

Cricket could see no reason not to tell him. 'I think you are right,' he said. 'But they'll have sent for help, you know.'

'As I told you, Crusher,' said Gainscorn smoothly. 'The Lord

Farwalker,' and he spoke Farwalker's title as if he had bitten on acid, 'is bound to come to her call. He'll have weapons enough.'

'So we get away before he arrives,' Crusher shouted at him. 'Here, Handy, you go up the hill there with a flag of truce and tell them we'll kill young hopeful here if they attack. If they let us go, with all our gear, we'll leave him behind, safe and sound. But we want her word on it, mind, Dragonfriend's.'

'Better say 'Wolftalker',' advised Gainscorn softly. 'That's what they call her. Do you want me to go too, to translate?'

'She'll be there. She can translate,' snapped Crusher. He glared at Gainscorn, his suspicion returning.

Gainscorn merely nodded. 'You're right. They'd probably kill me.'

Handy vanished between the folds of ground, trudging up the hill with an amber coloured rag tied to a stick held well up.

A couple of sentries went out and two more came in, saying that there was nothing to report, all was quiet.

Cricket was given some bread and a bowl of broth and tied on a long tether to a tree. The knots were so firmly tied that he didn't think he could have shifted them with his bare fingers even if they had not been well out of reach, between his shoulder blades. The other end of the tether was knotted round the tree higher than he could stretch.

Cricket was as safe as if he'd been locked in a vault, especially as there was always one of the outlaws guarding him. He thought that he might possibly have been able to get free if he'd been left alone long enough, perhaps, but…

Handy came back after a while looking bemused.

'They say they want to see the boy first,' he reported. 'If you take him out to the stream, they'll be able to see him, to be sure he's not hurt. Then they'll talk about letting us go.'

'Did you waste all this time on that?' roared Crusher. He seized Handy by the wrist and Handy screamed with pain and fell to his knees begging for mercy. Contemptuously, Crusher flung him away. 'Take the boy down to the stream,' he ordered.

The guard untied the rope from the tree, with some difficulty, and led Cricket to the water's edge. He looked up the hill, hoping to see someone, but there was no sign.

Handy was sent back to the parley. He returned, running.

'They're here! They got here already!' he gasped. 'The Borderers, and Lord Farwalker. I seen them!'

CHAPTER TWENTY-SEVEN

'What did Farwalker say?' Crusher shook his messenger violently and slapped his face. Handy gulped and pulled himself together.

'He said, Lord Farwalker said, "Your health depends on the health of your hostage. Send him to us now and we'll let you go free; but empty-handed. You take nothing with you." and then he says to me, he says, "Don't come back without the boy," and I'm not going to, I'm not!'

Crusher hit him again. 'You'll do as I tell you,' he said, almost indifferently. Then he turned to Cricket.

He was sitting on the ground at the foot of his tether tree, cross-legged in the storyteller fashion, trying to keep a little courage intact. Crusher gave him his bared teeth grin.

'It seems they're concerned for your health, storyteller,' he said, 'Perhaps we can make something of that. Let's see. What might be done and still leave you healthy? Storytellers do a lot of travelling, don't they? Eh, lad?' He gave him a nudge with his foot.

'Most of them do,' Cricket agreed, trying to sound indifferent.

'Sulking? That won't do.' Crusher nudged him again, harder. He kept still and tried not to show any fear, though there was sweat trickling clammily down his spine. 'Yes, storytellers do a lot of travelling. So they need their feet in good condition, hmm?'

'Yes, of course,' Cricket said.

'So suppose we lopped off a few of your toes?' Crusher beamed at him and the nudge became a kick, not very hard as yet.

'I'd rather you didn't,' Cricket told him; and was proud that his voice did not shake.

'Ah, but now that I think on it, storytellers have little carts to ride in, don't they? Don't they?' he repeated and Cricket nodded, shutting his eyes. This time the kick was hard enough to double him over, coughing. Crusher pulled him up by the hair. 'No, that won't do,' he said thoughtfully. 'I have it! You people like to wave your hands about as you gabble. We'll have off some fingers!'

Cricket looked down at his hands. The scar on the forefinger of his left hand, where the knife slipped as he shaved kindling wood, the crooked little fingers of both hands which he had so often wished straight, even the hangnail he had painfully peeled the day before were all suddenly most precious. He swallowed hard and stared up at Crusher's grin.

'Whatever you do,' Cricket said, amazed at his steady voice, 'will be repaid, with interest.'

Crusher's grin did not alter. 'If,' he said. Cricket frowned, puzzled.

'If I'm caught,' explained Crusher, amiably. 'But a man might as well be hanged for a horse as a foal, right? So why don't I send your quibbling friends a slice of your tongue? How's that for a notion, hey?'

Cricket's mouth went dry as if filled with ashes. The bile rose in the back of his throat and he tried to swallow, remembering with painful clarity Wolftalker telling how she had wet herself with terror when she first saw a Dragon at close quarters. He managed to hang on, just.

'Be polite to your host,' Crusher instructed him, with a sort of greed in his voice. Cricket realised that he had not answered Crusher and that he was hoping for another excuse to kick him. He was playing with him, Cricket knew, but the game had certain rules.

'It is a very silly notion,' he heard himself say with idiot confidence; and wondered what under Sky he could say next. His mind was blank.

'Huh? It'll show them I'm serious!' retorted Crusher, peering

156

down at him. Cricket's tongue seemed to be doing quite well on its own so he opened his mouth again.

'Damaged goods are worthless,' stated his voice and he suddenly saw what arguments to use. 'What earthly use is a storyteller who can't tell stories? What would you do if one of your men had a crippled hand and could no longer fight?'

Crusher frowned. 'I'd throw him out, of course. But I'm not like your mates; they won't throw you out. Wouldn't look good, would it, the great Lord Farwalker and the Overlord's pet storyteller letting her apprentice be ruined? No, they're not like me; they're soft.'

'So you'd expect them to give in if you told them you would –' Cricket licked dry lips with a dry tongue – 'cut bits off my tongue?' He held his breath. Would Crusher realise that Cricket had changed his proposed deed into a mere threat?

'That's right,' Crusher agreed cheerfully, 'I send old Handy back again and he tells them to let us go and all our gear or we send them their mate's tongue in slices. That'll fetch them.'

Gainscorn had been listening, frowning. Now he said, 'Handy's a fool. He'll mess it up somehow. Send someone else, for Sky's sake!'

Crusher shook his head. 'He's only to say what I tell him; and he don't know a thing more. So he's safe enough.'

'Yes, if they agree at once,' said Gainscorn slowly, twisting a twig between his fingers. 'But suppose they make conditions, set a trap for us? Handy would never see it! I don't care to trust my life to his wits, especially when he's scared out of most of them!'

'You don't, hey? Then you can go yourself!' snapped Crusher, irritated.

Cricket saw Gainscorn's hands relax, though his face did not change. The twig fell to the ground as he began a feeble protest. Crusher swept it aside vigorously. Gainscorn should go, he would have no argument. But Cricket was sure that Gainscorn had intended to be the messenger all along.

Gainscorn came back sooner than Cricket had expected. Handy had taken much longer. Had Gainscorn hurried or were Wolftalker and Farwalker nearer? He peered hopefully up the slope even though he knew he couldn't possibly see them. Crusher was hopping with impatience even so.

'What do they say?' he shouted as soon as Gainscorn was within earshot. Gainscorn made him wait. He sat down by the fire, automatically crossed his legs then hastily uncrossed them and said: 'They want guarantees!' in a disgusted voice.

Crusher looked blank. 'Guarantees? What of?' he asked.

'Of young clodpole's safety, of course. What else?' asked Gainscorn wearily.

'Do you mean they think I won't cut out his tongue...' began Crusher, spluttering with rage. Gainscorn cut him short.

'I have convinced them that you mean business,' he said, 'and that the boy is unhurt – so far! They are afraid you'll harm him after they have let you go. What they want – and I told them I was sure you'd never agree to it – is for you to leave the boy behind, tied to the tree just the way he is now.' He paused significantly. 'Farwalker said that his word is good and yours is not.'

There was a dangerous silence. Gainscorn looked at Cricket and looked away again, blankly. The outlaws shuffled and tried not to catch Crusher's eye. Cricket glanced at him and was suddenly bubbling with frightened laughter. He had gone purple with rage. Cricket had never before believed that people actually went that colour.

Crusher let out his held breath in a huge bellow of fury, wordless and terrifying, then began to curse Farwalker. When he had repeated himself twice, Gainscorn broke in, raising his voice above Crusher's. 'Do you wish to send him a reply? Or are we back where we started?'

For a moment Cricket thought Crusher would pull a knife on Gainscorn but with an effort he controlled himself and stood panting. 'How many men were there?' he asked.

Gainscorn shrugged. 'I saw a score, Wilders and Borderers mixed. There may have been more, hidden; very likely there were. How could I tell? There were five or six wolves in view which means there are certainly more of them. There was also a foreigner, a soft looking type, no warrior, that's for sure.'

Cricket felt a wave of relief. That must be Cloud. He was safe, after all. Gainscorn must have noticed his expression for he said sharply, 'You know something of this foreigner, clodpole?' and Crusher at once turned on Cricket threateningly.

'He was with us, me and Wolftalker,' Cricket stammered. He did not need to pretend fear. 'We got separated and I thought he might have been hurt.' He could not see that it mattered if they knew this. It would do them no good and Cloud no harm.

Gainscorn wanted to know more but he asked the wrong questions, curious as to where Cloud had joined them and why, and Cricket answered with the exact truth and no more. If he told them that Cloud had said he wanted adventure, he need not add that Wolftalker had ideas about Cloud's other possible reasons; or that she and Lord Farwalker had both quarrelled with him.

They left the subject at last. More important was the question of Cricket being left behind. Gainscorn did not say in so many words that Crusher could trust Lord Farwalker; but he made it obvious that he was in favour of leaving him.

'The boy will slow us down,' he pointed out. 'And we shall have to travel fast to outdistance rumour. You know what will happen to us if word gets out about the gildentrees before we can disguise ourselves and change our identities. Cut your losses, Crusher. Forget the boy and run!'

Crusher shook his head, like a bull tormented with flies. 'Go back and tell the Archer that if he pushes me I'll take my revenge on the boy.'

'He knows it!' Gainscorn almost lost control. 'I told him and he believed me. For the Stars' sake, Crusher, let's go!'

Crusher hesitated. 'We'll start tomorrow at dawn,' he said sullenly. 'Go and tell them, Storyteller.'

Gainscorn, who had turned to climb the slope again, whipped round, the blood draining from his face. 'Don't call me that!' he whispered with such fury that Cricket was not surprised when Crusher took a pace back from him and laughed uneasily.

Gainscorn stood as if waiting for Crusher to answer him, then, as Crusher did not speak, he flung round and fairly ran up the hill. It struck Cricket that Crusher had made another enemy.

CHAPTER TWENTY-EIGHT

The rest of the day was spent by the outlaws in packing their possessions, disputing over loot and arguing about where they were to go. Very few of them wanted to stay with Crusher.

To Cricket's surprise, Gainscorn tried to persuade them to stick together. Crusher, he argued, was a good leader and worth three men if it came to a fight. They might have Farwalker's promise not to pursue them, but once word spread of what they had done, there would be no safe place to hide. They must get out of the country and keep going as fast and as far as possible. With luck they could pass themselves off as a group of warriors for hire but only if they stayed together.

Cricket saw that Handy was listening closely. Presently he strolled away to where Crusher's tent stood, looked around carefully and then ducked furtively inside.

'Say we do stick with Crusher,' said one of the men, 'Where do we go?'

'We haven't a lot of choice,' Gainscorn told him, 'and I think,' he added sharply, 'we'd do well to discuss it out of our friend's hearing!'

He indicated Cricket by walking over and kicking his ankle. He jerked away and Gainscorn bent over the boy to check the knots at his back. 'Seems firm enough,' he remarked, tugging at the tether. 'Don't fret; you'll soon be free, clodhopper. One way or another,' he added and looked Cricket straight in the eye, repeating softly, 'One way or another!'

Cricket stared after him, not knowing whether to hope or fear.

Why was Crusher so reluctant to run? Was there, as the High

Overlord's message had said, more behind the destruction of the gildentrees than greed? Was Wolfbane's plot against Graycat still working? Did the outlaws really not yet know that Wolfbane was dead?

Gainscorn knew, surely – or did he? Should Cricket say anything about it to them? He couldn't decide. Presently the man guarding him, who had been staring at him for some time, said in a low voice: 'You ever seen the Overlord, Storyteller?'

'D'you mean Graycat? Or Overlord Strongmind? I've seen them both,' Cricket told him.

'Her – Graycat! What's she like, really?'

'Tall. Thin. Not pretty, but you keep looking at her.' He thought for a moment. 'Gainscorn has seen her. Has he never talked about her?'

'Him! He wouldn't give a bad word to a dog! Got a tongue like a razor and likes to use it.'

'And Head, of course, barely saw her when he and Leg and Shoulder attacked her on the road,' Cricket said, watching him cautiously. Was there any hope of talking this one round? But he was no Wolftalker, to coax enemies into well-wishers in minutes.

'That's right. Head don't talk much anyroad. Did she speak to you, ever?'

'Yes. After all, I am Storyteller Wolftalker Dragonfriend's own apprentice,' Cricket said proudly, 'and she is Overlord Graycat's own Storyteller and Remembrancer. The Lady has spoken to me – oh, several times. She is always very gracious and often merry. She loves to laugh. But I hope never to cross her.'

The outlaw nodded thoughtfully. Then he leaned nearer and spoke more softly. 'What do you reckon she'll do if old Crusher does – you know?' and he made a throat cutting gesture.

Cricket gulped. 'She's Graycat. What do you think?'

The man made the sign against ill luck. 'Let's hope Gainscorn can talk Crusher round, hey?'

'How did Gainscorn come to join you?' Cricket asked, idly.

He was not eager to think about Crusher's intentions.

'Dunno, really. He just turned up one day. Crusher knew him, said he brought a message from the City and now we could get on with the job. So that's what we did.'

'Felling the gildentrees,' Cricket nodded.

'We got leave! That was the message!'

Cricket shook his head. 'I think the message was something else; if so, Crusher lied to you. The Overlord Strongmind's death made it impossible for the message to be true, you see. It was he who was supposed to have given you leave, not Graycat. Now, if the person who was employing you told Gainscorn that you had leave, he lied; and Gainscorn, who knew of the Overlord's death before he left the City, would have known it was a lie. So I don't think that was the message. Gainscorn is still too much of a storyteller to lie outright.'

The guard dropped his voice still lower. 'Was he a real storyteller? He's never said. Crusher said he was, and then Gainscorn half killed the man that asked him to tell us a tale! No one dared ask again.'

Cricket supposed that he could have kept the conversation on Graycat or perhaps turned it to Wolftalker and maybe he ought to have. But he still wanted to know how much the outlaws had been told about what they were doing. So, keeping almost to a whisper, he told the outlaw what had happened to Gaingold to turn him into Gainscorn.

'It's no wonder he hates me,' he finished. 'I hated him for long enough; and, to his way of thinking, I destroyed him. Though the Stars know he brought it on himself.'

'Even so you reckon he wouldn't lie to us?'

'He wouldn't. Storytellers born have it drummed into them from the moment they can understand speech,' Cricket reminded him. 'Now me, I'm not born to it. I have to stop and think. But Gainscorn was born to it. He might twist the truth a bit, but he can't lie, not the way you or I might.'

He wondered how much he was spoiling Gainscorn's plans, if plans he had; but there was one thing Cricket had to know. 'Do you know who sent the message by Gainscorn?' he asked, trying to sound as though he had no idea himself.

'It won't matter if I tell you,' said the man, carelessly. 'It's over now, anyway. Yes, it was some lord with a queer name... sort of name you might give a huntsman or a bowman... Wolfbane! That was it! Well, now that you know, if Crusher leaves you behind you'll be able to tell the lords, won't you! Do you a bit of good, hey?'

He gave Cricket a gap-toothed grin and he smiled back as neutrally as he could. It was obvious that the man had no idea that Wolfbane had been exposed and had killed himself.

Should Cricket tell him? Would it make any difference now? How would Crusher react? Cricket was scared to do anything which might change the delicate balance on which his life hung. He wished he knew whether Gainscorn had heard of Wolfbane's downfall or not. He must decide quickly, now, at once, whether to speak or keep silent.

He kept silent. The risk was too great. If he told them, although logically they would then have less reason to harm him, Crusher would realise that they had not been stumbled upon by chance and his first thought would be to revenge himself on Cricket. Gainscorn would never be able to stand against Crusher's fury. And still Cricket did not know what Gainscorn knew or what he meant to do.

The afternoon wore on slowly, slowly. Nobody bothered to feed him and at last he curled up in the warm sun to forget his hunger in sleep.

CHAPTER TWENTY-NINE

Cricket woke suddenly with a gasp of alarm. Someone was shaking him, a hand over his mouth.

Gainscorn!

He tried to shrink away and Gainscorn whispered, 'Fool! Keep still and silent.'

A knife glinted in the dim light. It was not yet full dark but Cricket could not see his face against the red of the sunset. He froze and the knife slid to the tether, sliced, and Cricket was free. He gathered his feet beneath him cautiously.

Gainscorn tugged at his wrist and Cricket obeyed, creeping after him with the utmost delicacy past the snoring shape of the guard and down the slope, away from the camp, where most of the outlaws were gathered. He could hear their voices and see a fire glowing in the twilight.

There was no sign of the sentry Cricket knew was on the watch somewhere nearby and Gainscorn was moving faster and more confidently. Cricket peered anxiously around and almost tripped over a sprawled mass at his feet. He stopped, teetering off balance. Gainscorn grabbed his arm.

'He can't hear you,' he hissed impatiently. 'I stunned him. Come on, boy – hurry! Curse this light. It took me too long to stalk him.' He glanced behind them nervously as they approached the edge of the trees.

'Why?' Cricket asked him.

'Why did I release you? They've decided to kill you and sneak away as soon as it is dark. I told Wolftalker I'd help you if I could, clodhopper, if it got to that point. Word of a storyteller!' He gave a snort of bitter amusement. 'I told Crusher he'd be a fool to kill you and that –' he used a word Cricket did not recognise, his knowledge of the Elder tongue being still limited '–struck me. Me!' His hand went to his face and he snatched it away again. Cricket knew that he had not touched the bruise when the blow was delivered: he would have taken it indifferently and made no protest. This was his protest.

'I must have your oath never to tell what that gabble monger told you about Wolfbane,' he added. 'Balancing one promise against another gets tricky.'

'No need,' Cricket panted. 'He's dead. Killed himself when the Overlord found out his plot.'

They were among the trees now and in almost complete darkness, so Cricket could not see the expression on his face; but to his surprise Gainscorn laughed softly and said, 'How ironic! So I need not have worried about where my loyalties lay. No, I'd have released you anyway. We can't have the peasants thinking they can kill a storyteller, can we? But revenge sweetens the deed.'

They were shuffling forward unable to see any way at all when Cricket stumbled upon a thread of path running between the bushes. They followed it in single file, moving as fast as they dared. When Cricket slowed, trying to move quietly, Gainscorn pushed him on urgently.

'Speed is more important now than silence. Your guard is due to be relieved at any moment.'

'You aren't going back to them, then,' Cricket said, stupidly.

'No, clodpole, I am not. If we get out alive I shall have to depend solely upon your gratitude, shan't I?' Gainscorn gave a derisive sniff and halted. Cricket stopped too. A distant cry of alarm sounded behind them.

'Run!' snapped Gainscorn; and they fled.

The trees were a little sparser here but the light was now so dim that their footing was just as treacherous; still, they pounded along the narrow path, ducking low branches and hurdling bushes. Somehow they both kept their feet. Then the path forked. Cricket skidded to a halt and Gainscorn crashed into him, sending him staggering.

'Which way?' Cricket gasped.

'Left. No, right. Make better time downhill,' he panted. Cricket realised with a shock of fear that he did not know where the path would take them.

'No!' he said. 'Stop. Think. Which way takes us quickest to the Wilders?'

Gainscorn shoved him on towards the right hand path. 'Any way. They're all around. And Farwalker and his Borderers, too. Get on, boy!' They ran on.

At the bottom of the slope they burst out of the trees into a grassy valley. There was enough light left in the sky to see where a stream ran fast and stonily down the middle and, on its far side, a much steeper hill.

There the trees were far apart, offering very little cover. Gainscorn hesitated, looking right and left anxiously. Cricket saw movement on the brow of the ridge facing them and pointed it out to him. 'Isn't that the Wilders? Look, up there!'

Gainscorn nodded eagerly and they ran down to the stream and splashed hastily across. Too hastily, for Cricket trod on a weed covered stone and fell helplessly into the stream, his left ankle trapped between two rocks.

Gainscorn scooped him up at once; but when he tried to walk, his ankle gave way and he fell again, a lightning flash of pain up his leg driving all thought from him for the moment. Then Gainscorn was half carrying, half dragging him up the slope, cursing breathlessly. Cricket's left arm was draped over his shoulder and he held the boy painfully round the waist, heaving his dangling body forward as he staggered awkwardly along.

For a while Cricket could not speak for pain, but he groaned and tried to use his legs. Gainscorn stopped, propped them both against a tree and gasped for breath.

'Stars, you're a weight, boy. Can you walk?'

Cricket tried to stand on his own and almost fell. He felt terribly sick and dizzy and he must have looked it, for Gainscorn peered at him and said, 'No, I see you can't. Moon and Stars, I'll have to carry you now, you clumsy clodhopper. Here, on my back. Put your arms around my neck and hang on tight. I can't spare a hand to hold you.'

Cricket clung on, trying not to choke him and they moved on again. The slope was very steep here and Gainscorn went up it almost on all fours, grunting with the effort and Cricket's weight.

There was a shout below them and then a long hunting call. Crusher's men had spotted them.

'Fools!' Gainscorn gasped. 'Telling the Borderers where they are! Where we are, too,' and struggled on.

Another call sounded from above them, away to the left, then a horn, fierce and exultant. Farwalker's call!

'Let's wait here for the Borderers,' Cricket suggested hopefully. 'They'll soon find us.'

'No!' Gainscorn panted, 'Crusher! He'll be coming – daren't stop.'

Cricket's foot throbbed with every jolting step and he longed to stop and rest. 'He must know he can't catch us now,' he protested.

'Can still kill us. Revenge,' grunted Gainscorn, weaving from tree to tree. Cricket knew that he feared an arrow or a crossbow quarrel and was trying to shelter them behind the tree trunks. But the trees were very slender here and gave them little cover.

'I'll get down. Let you run for it,' Cricket said, loosening his grasp. 'He won't bother about me.'

Gainscorn grabbed his wrists fiercely. 'Will. I know him. Stay put,' he ordered.

There was a yell from below. 'I see you, Gainscorn, you treacher! I'll have you now! First your minion, then you!'

And Gainscorn flung himself round to face Crusher's arrow.

Cricket actually saw it coming. Farwalker said later that he couldn't have, not in that light; but he did. It slammed into Gainscorn's chest and he staggered back, still holding Cricket's wrists, then fell sideways. Cricket fell with him, just saving his foot from his weight and they lay entangled on the slope, slipping down it gradually until a slim birch tree stopped them.

But before they even began to slide there was a dreadful scream from below and Gainscorn muttered breathlessly, 'Crusher's dead. That's Farwalker's work, Cricket.'

His hands slackened and Cricket tried to cushion him as they slid; but he slipped away from him. It was the first time he had called Cricket by name.

Voices called from above them and Cricket tried to shout. He could only croak but someone heard and there was a great crashing as several people scrambled recklessly down the hill.

A moment later Drinks-the-Wind was licking his face and Wolftalker was sliding down beside him.

'Gainscorn!' Cricket said to them. 'He's hurt. He took the arrow meant for me. Help him!'

Wolftalker turned to the Wilders who had followed her down.

'We'll need stretchers for them both,' she said. 'Will you cut the poles, Oakshadow? And one of you fetch Healer Foxglove as quickly as you can.'

She pulled a water bottle from her belt and tried to give Gainscorn a drink. Cricket made to get up to go to them but a Wilder pushed him gently down again. 'Sit still, the healer is coming,' he said.

Gainscorn feebly thrust the bottle away. 'Don't bother,' he said. 'The healer can't help me, either.' He coughed and retched.

The Wilder murmured, 'He's coughing blood. It got his lung,' and someone else said, with finality, 'He's dying.'

Wolftalker said clearly, 'Gaingold Storyteller, will you give to me your Story?' and there was an awed hush.

The faint voice said, 'That's not my name. Lost my Name.'

'I, Storyteller Wolftalker Dragonfriend, give you back your Name and Title; and will maintain your right to both before all the storytellers in the Land,' said Wolftalker firmly. 'This do I swear on my Guild Oath and by my Names. May I live Nameless else.'

Cricket shuddered at the thought of what echoes this terrible oath must raise for her; but Gaingold actually chuckled. Then he coughed tearingly. When he could speak again he gasped, 'Can't see. Is the boy safe?'

This time Cricket didn't let anyone stop him. He got to his knees somehow and crawled forward. 'I'm here,' he told him, 'I'm fine. You saved me, Gaingold. I owe you my life.'

Gaingold nodded. 'Give you my Story,' he said weakly. 'Not her. You. Tell it right, Cricket Storyteller,' and he coughed and coughed again and the blood filled his mouth and he was dead.

Cricket crouched there, staring stupidly. Presently, sheltered by the darkness, he wept.

CHAPTER THIRTY

Cricket's time with the Wilders was put off until he had finished working on the Story of Gaingold. He was sent to stay with Storyteller Spring Rain so that she might help him, for he felt completely overwhelmed by the responsibility, even though Wolftalker assured him that he could do a workmanlike job.

'Gaingold was clever,' she said, rather grudgingly. 'He knew you'd try harder than anyone else in the Joined Lands to do him justice. Don't wear yourself out, that's all. You are still my apprentice, remember. I don't want people like Shellgather saying what a pity it is I don't know how to treat you!'

It was not too difficult to tell the Story of the journey and their experiences with the outlaws. Cricket told it to Spring Rain's friends and relatives when he reached Brownhill. He left out any mention of the Fellowship, of course, just gave them a straightforward account of what happened.

One of the relatives, a Master Storyteller, made an unkind remark about Wolftalker's having left Cricket to face Crusher alone. Cricket knew he had made it clear how little choice she'd had; and he remembered her face when she found him again. So he said, coldly, 'I am still her apprentice.' and the man stiffened and bowed to him. And apologised!

Cricket told Spring Rain everything, excepting only what Wolftalker had told him of her love for Farwalker. She had not asked him not to speak of it; she had simply trusted him and he would not fail her. But everything else, including his own very mixed feelings about Gaingold, Cricket told her.

She was a member of the Fellowship, so he could even tell her about that; and how, as he had learned during his brief stay in the City on their return, Graycat had sent Carter Stark to talk sense into the disaffected members of the Fellowship who had been told lies by Wolfbane's agents. Cricket rather suspected Stark of knocking a few heads together as well as talking, Stark being Stark; but she had come back cheerfully triumphant and Graycat had asked no questions.

The most entertaining part of Cricket's account was about Cloud. Wolftalker had guessed, quite correctly, that the reason he had been unable to get on with Farwalker was simply jealousy.

He had fallen in love with Graycat himself. But Wolftalker admitted that she had not for one moment suspected what the High Overlord's herald, distraught with worry, revealed as they all straggled into the Great House, tired and grubby and, in Cricket's case, half carried between Speedhand and Cloud.

The herald had run forward, forgetting all his stateliness to fall on his knees before Cloud, crying, 'Oh, my dear lord! Thank the Stars you are safe, Skyfriend!'

The High Overlord himself grinned ruefully at his herald and said, 'You might have waited until I'd changed into something more suitable, my friend.'

The herald's anxiety after their departure had long since led Graycat to suspect who Cloud was. She did not resent having been deceived; indeed she seemed rather to admire Cloud for it and to be considerably amused.

She and Cloud Skyfriend were to be married the following spring, in the High Overlord's own city, much to the annoyance of the citizens of her own capital, particularly Strongtower, Lord of the Streetskimmers, for whom no city could compare with his.

Wolftalker would go with the wedding party as a matter of course and Cricket had been invited by Skyfriend himself as a return favour, he said, for the oatcakes and water Cricket had once brought him. Cricket found that he still liked him very much, as he told Rain, in spite of having been fooled by him.

Cricket also told Rain about Wolftalker's unwitting use of The Voice, and of his own clumsiness in pressing her about it.

Rain patted his hand. 'Never mind, Cricket; you had been given a bad shock and were not yourself. Young Wolftalker Dragonfriend will have to forgive herself for losing her first Storyteller Name eventually and then she will be able to admit she is Talented. She's a brave lass but that is something not many can face easily. It may be easier for her when she weds.'

'Weds?' Cricket was dumbstruck. 'When she weds? But what – who do you mean?'

'Why, the one she loves, of course! Farwalker! Oh, Cricket, Farwalker loves her. Have you not seen it?'

Cricket sat with his mouth half open, remembering Wolftalker's outburst. *That's all right then*, he thought, but managed not to say.

Rain laughed gently at his expression. 'Leave that for now, He scarcely knows himself yet. Go on, my dear, what happened next with that dreadful Crusher?'

So Cricket told her how terrified he had been of Crusher's cruelty. 'I didn't know anybody could be like that. He just slammed into anyone who even looked like disagreeing with him! I'd no idea what to do… I kept thinking of things to say but none of them were any good… and then – and then – Gainscorn! Suddenly he seemed to be Gaingold again! I don't understand how he could help Crusher and his men try to pull down Graycat? And then save me… with his own body…

'How can I tell his Story if I can't understand him?' he asked Rain.

She nodded. 'It is as if he were two men,' she said seriously. 'Gaingold helped you while Gainscorn hated you.'

Cricket thought about it while she sat silent, giving him space to come to his own conclusions.

Presently Cricket said, 'While I was in the City, before my foot was well enough for me to come to Brownhill, I talked to everyone I could who had known Gaingold. There were two different accounts of him. Most people said he was very cynical and sharp, with an eye to the main chance, but some said he could be kind, but was easily hurt and hid it by acting the cynic. Do you think someone could pretend cynicism until it became a real but separate part of him? I'm not saying this clearly; I don't really know quite what I do mean,' he confessed, rubbing his face in confusion, 'but, well, one of the things Gaingold said, that we couldn't have Crusher thinking he could kill storytellers, when he was explaining why he'd saved me...'

'You think that was true? Or his pretended cynicism?'

'I think he meant it; and at the same time it was pretence. After all, he spent long enough saying I wasn't worthy to be a storyteller, back at Edgescarp, and in the hearing and – and then, he called *me* storyteller, he protected me *as* a storyteller, and he gave *me* his Story.' Cricket sighed.

Storyteller Spring Rain chuckled. 'Now, I'll tell you a storyteller trick, young Cricket,' she said, her voice warm with laughter. 'When there is something you don't understand in a story, just tell it as it happened and let your listeners tell you what it means. They'll love to! And they will think more highly of you if you don't explain everything.'

So since Cricket could think of nothing better, he agreed to tell Gaingold's Story like that: as a mystery. And perhaps Gaingold would have enjoyed being a puzzle for as long as his story would be told. Until, as the storyteller rhyme has it, the world's end.

'Though sticks or stones may break your bones,
Those bones with care will mend;
But the storyteller's Name for you
Clings fast to your life's end;
And the Story that they tell of you
May last till the world's end.'

Follow us on Twitter
@ArachnePress @SolShorts

Like us on Facebook
ArachnePress, SolsticeShorts2014

arachnepress.com

More Books by Ghillian Potts
from Arachne Press
arachnepress.com

Brat: Book One of *The Naming of Brook Storyteller*
by Ghillian Potts
ISBN: 978-1-909208-41-4
On her twelfth birthday Brat's father disappears. She waits, but he never comes back. Reduced to begging and determined to find out what has happened to him, she is helped by Gray and Baylock, whom she quickly discovers are outlaws. Brat finds that nothing is simple, nowhere is safe, and being reunited with her family must wait, as more pressing tasks fall into her path.

Spellbinder: Book Two of *The Naming of Brook Storyteller*
by Ghillian Potts
ISBN: 978-1-909208-46-9
Brook, now called Spellbinder, is working as Remembrancer to her friend Graycat, now the Young Overlord Lady Quicksilver, when Storytellers start disappearing. Spellbinder is captured and forced to summon the Elder Dragons, but when she cannot control them, she must break her Storyteller vow and forfeit her most precious possession – her name.

The Old Woman from Friuli
by Ghillian Potts, illustrated by Ed Boxall
ISBN: 978-1-909208-40-7
The Duke looks out from his castle, and everything he can see for miles and miles belongs to him. Everything, except one small strong house, with a small garden, two goats and a beehive. *They* belong to the old woman from Friuli. The Duke wants that house, but the old woman, she won't sell. She's from Friuli, where all the *really* stubborn people come from.